Kate Harrington

Centennial and Other Poems

Kate Harrington

Centennial and Other Poems

ISBN/EAN: 9783744711814

Printed in Europe, USA, Canada, Australia, Japan

Cover: Foto ©Andreas Hilbeck / pixelio.de

More available books at **www.hansebooks.com**

(From portrait taken in 1854)

Kate Harrington.

CENTENNIAL

AND

OTHER POEMS.

BY

KATE HARRINGTON.

DO YOU LOVE POETRY?

Do you love poetry? When o'er your spirit
  Shadows of grief and of care slowly steal,
Do the low whispers which some souls inherit
  Beautiful thoughts to your fancy reveal?
Oh! if this be so, though sometimes earth-weary,
  Life is not always unchangingly real,
Like to a desert, all lonely and dreary,
  Having no gleams of the lovely Ideal.

If you love poetry, sorrow and sadness,
  Mountains of cares and afflictions may throng,
Yet will your spirit leap up in her gladness
  When strains burst forth from the fountain of **song**.
For there is something within us adoring,—
  Something no mortal has ever defined,
Raising us upward whene'er we are poring
  Over these mystical dreams of the mind.

PHILADELPHIA:

J. B. LIPPINCOTT & CO.

1876.

DEDICATION.

IOWA.

Upon the breast of Iowa
  An honored sire reposes;
And o'er a sainted mother's clay
  Blossom her summer roses.
My eldest darling passed, this way,
  Up, through the portals pearly;
A blue-eyed baby, too, they lay
  Beneath the violets early.

Where erst the red man's bow was bent,
  Beside our noble river,
An elder brother rests content,
  In home and hearthstone, ever.
An only sister keeps, like me,
  Watch where her first-born slumbers;
And lists in vain, on bended knee,
  To catch her waking numbers.

'Twas here I bent, a blighted vine,
  A bruised reed, well-nigh broken,

3

Till kindly hands were clasped in mine,
  And cheering words were spoken.
And 'tis for this my heart would stay,—
  My soul, till death, would hover
Near friends who stood beside the flood
  When love and life passed over.

I pledge my songs to Iowa,
  If they to effort nerve her;
I pledge my heart to Iowa
  Whenc'er my love may serve her.
'Twas here my marriage-vows were given,—
  'Twas here my children found me;
My home is here, and here may Heaven
  Fold angel-wings around me.

Then join my prayer for Iowa;
  May valiant sons defend her!
And may her daughters give alway
  Their love, warm, true, and tender!
May sacred memories hold us here,
  And, till Life's brief dream closes,
May we her name, her soil revere,
  And sleep beneath her roses!

TABLE OF CONTENTS.

IOWA'S CENTENNIAL POEM.

A HUNDRED years ago to-day
A barren wild our borders lay;
Our stately forests grandly stood
Wrapped in majestic solitude.
Our rivers, coursing to the sea,
Felt not the chain of tyranny;
Nor yet above their glittering sheen
Could Freedom's stripes and stars be seen.

The red man moored his birch canoe
Where sweet wild-flowers luxuriant grew;
Where sumachs, o'er the pebbly brink,
Bent down their crimson lips to drink;
And violets, with their tender eyes,
Looked up in wondering surprise
At Indian maid, who, by the wave,
Waited to greet her warrior brave.

A hundred years! Gone like a dream,
All, save our woods and noble stream;

A*

9

The red man, with his bended bow,
No longer fells the bounding doe.
The camp-fire's curling smoke no more
Is seen beside the chieftain's door,
As Black Hawk talks, in whispers grave,
To Gitchie Manito the Brave.
But on this broad, luxuriant plain
Wave golden fields of ripening grain ;
Our pastures, with their gurgling rills,
Feed cattle on a thousand hills,
While giant steamers plow our streams,
From which our starry banner gleams.
The mansions on our prairies wide,
Oft with a rude cot by their side,
Show how, by years of patient toil,
The lordly tillers of our soil
Have reared such homes as freemen may
With all their shackles torn away.

The flying shuttle, whirling wheel,
Invention's mighty power reveal.
We sweep, by steam, o'er earth's broad track,
And lightning sends our whispers back.
We share the nation's glory, too,
By holding to the world's broad view

Our men of mark, of genius rare,
Scattered, like sunbeams, everywhere.

On history's page will shine most bright
Such names as Belknap, Kirkwood, Wright,
Howell, McCreary, Mason, Hall,
Dodge, faithful to his country's call,
And warriors who, through war's wild shock,
Anchored our ship on Union rock.

The call that rose at Lexington,
Where Freedom's struggle was begun,
Reached not these shores, yet still we claim
This priceless heritage the same.
They were our ancestors who fought
When liberty with blood was bought.
And Concord, with her patriot band,
Whose sons to-day rejoicing stand,
Deserves no more the honors won
Than we, so near the setting sun.

Could our hearts bound with wilder thrill
If we had met on Bunker's Hill?
Are patriots truer on the sod
Whence those brave souls went up to God?

Not if, with loyal heart and hand,
We held the heritage they planned ;
Not if, along this verdant track,
When Dissolution's cloud hung black,
Our soldiers poured their blood like rain,—
Deluged our sod with crimson stain,—
And flung our starry banner out
With glad, prolonged victorious shout,
Proclaiming where its bright folds waved
Our fathers' boon—the Union—saved.

Yes, side by side with those who sped
Where'er the gallant Putnam led,
With those whose forms grew cold and still
Upon the brow of Bunker's Hill,
We proudly write, on History's page,
The heroes of the present age ;
Our dauntless braves, who did not quail
Beneath the storm of iron hail,
But who, like valiant Warren, fell
Guarding the land they loved so well.

Mills, Baker, Torrence, Worthington,
Martyrs to Freedom dearly won,
Beside their tombs our patriots cry,
"As much of valor as *could* die!"

Ask ye if Woman shrinking stood,
When rang War's cry o'er field and flood?
Did mothers, racked by dire alarms,
Prison their sons with clinging arms?
No; worthy of the patriot sires
That lit the Revolution fires,
They forced the tears, that needs must start,
Backward, *to trickle through the heart*,
And said, in accents firm and low,
"Our prayers will follow,—go, boys, go!"

So when ye boast, as boast ye will,
Of the green slopes of Bunker's Hill,
And vow that ne'er shall be forgot
How Shiloh and Pea Ridge were fought;
When, with fond pride, you teach your son
How Tuttle's men took Donelson;
When to Alltoona you refer,
And tell how Corse defended her;
Or when you link with Archer's name
The sword his son will proudly claim,
Forget not Woman, who, through tears,
Read how the form that other years
Had seen soft-pillowed on her breast,—
The lips her own so fondly pressed

Had murmured forth their dying moan—
Had paled and chilled, unsoothed—alone,—
Remember, every gallant one
Who fell was some fond mother's son.

I stood beneath our State's proud dome,
And saw the dear old Flag* come home.
Weary and worn and well-nigh spent,
To you, O statesmen ! it was sent,
To hold as a more priceless gem
Than England's royal diadem.
On shattered staff the wounded bars
Held feebly up the golden stars,
While the scarred veteran seemed to say,
" E'en *death* is sweet in Iowa."

I fancied, as they bore it by,
Its red stripes glowed with deeper dye,
Since it had cheered each patriot one
Whose life-blood crimsoned Donelson.
Purer its lines of spotless white
Since trusting mothers knelt at night,
Lifting their yearning souls above
On the white wings of Faith and Love,

---

* Flag of the Iowa Second, General J. M. Tuttle, commander.

Pleading His arm might be the stay
Of valiant hearts from Iowa.

Deeper its blue since dimming eyes
Had faintly smiled in sweet surprise
Upon the silken folds that spread
Their pitying shadows o'er the dead,—
The loyal dead, for whom 'twas meet
Their Flag should be their winding-sheet.

Brighter its stars of deathless sheen
Since it had waved o'er fields of green,
Floated where giant steamers sailed,
Swayed—trembled—reeled—yet *never trailed.*

Well may we celebrate this day
  With glad, triumphant shout ;
Well may we bid dull care "Away,"
  And fling our banners out.
E'en Nature joins the welcome sounds
  By grateful hearts begun,
Till from our rocks and vales rebounds
  The name of Washington.

England her Wellington may claim ;
  France of Napoleon boast ;

Scotia extol the deathless fame
  Of Wallace and his host ;
But more ecstatic is the thrill
  That fires Columbia's son,
When lip and voice grow strangely still
  At thought of Washington.

Perchance e'en now the shades of those
  Who first in battle led
Have left their Eden of repose
  To hover o'er our head.
They were the sowers of the seed
  That made our country free,
And we, the reapers, loud indeed
  May shout forth " Victory !"

Nor to the arm of flesh alone
  Attribute our success ;
But to the One who led us on—
  The God who deigned to bless.
And while, to-day, our banners wave
  For battles dearly won,
We bless the power that victory gave
  To our own Washington.

Bought with the life-blood of the brave,
  Held through dissension's shock,

The heritage our fathers gave
  Stands firm on Freedom's rock.
Then send your welcomes near and far,
  Let party discord cease ;
And learn of him who, first in War,
  Was first alike in Peace.

Yes, patriot brothers, awaken !
  Leave the red field of carnage behind ;
Be former contentions forsaken,
  And thus prove all brave hearts are kind.
Would ye make this, our glorious Centennial,
  A type of the Union above?
Then join in our earthly millennial,
  And crown it with brotherly love.

Oh, be not by prejudice blinded !
  Our wanderers had something to learn ;
And by parable all are reminded
  That e'en prodigal sons may return.
Then let generous welcomes be proffered ;
  Give them robes of a right royal hue ;
Let the rings that restore them be offered
  By victors who honor the Blue.

They have desolate hearthstones among them,
  And hearts that still moan in their pain,
When the thought of the anguish that wrung them
  Floats over remembrance again.
Then when come your tear-drops, upstarting,
  For friends who passed over the tide,
Forget not that many a parting
  Brought woe on the Southern side.

In the names of our patriots ascended ;
  In the names of our heroes who bled ;
By the cause they so nobly defended ;
  By the Rachels who moaned o'er our dead ;
We ask you to pledge them, true-hearted,
  A covenant-promise anew ;
Remembering 'mong patriots departed
  No line parts the Gray from the Blue.

MOTHER.

In the voyage of life, 'mid its tempest and gale,
The glow of one beacon has never grown pale;
It burst into flame at the hour of my birth,
And has since been the brightest, most steadfast on earth.
Other beamings, illusive, might lure to betray,
Other flames, evanescent, might smoulder away,
But the light that from infancy brightened and blessed
Was the love of the mother now called to her Rest.

Oh, the welcoming arms with their tender embrace,
The glance of affection that lighted her face,
The lips that so often have opened in prayer
That my feet might be guarded from pitfall and snare,—
All have passed from my sight, and are hidden away
In the gloom that encircles the spiritless clay;
But the soul,—the immortal,—released from its bars,
Has laid down life's burden and leapt to the stars,

19

Where the dear mother-love, all undimmed, unrepressed,
Will be ours again when we enter our Rest.

'Tis a comforting thought that earth's pathway was trod
From the morn of her life, with the people of God ;
That when sorrow was deepest—when death sought her
    fold—
She reached up her hand for the Father to hold.
And we know that He clasped it, for, strengthened and
    sure,
Her faith made her feel in His promise secure
To the humble believer ; and long patient years
Of suffering were spent without doubtings or fears ;
And when, in Life's twilight, she asked for release,
When, wearied, she prayed that her waiting might cease,
The Saviour reached down as she slept on my breast,
Unloosened her fetters, and called her to Rest.

So quietly, softly, the summons was given,
We knew not our loss till the portals of heaven
Had oped to receive her, and waiting ones there
Had greeted her coming with anthem and prayer.
And she—oh ! she felt not our throbbings of pain,
Nor marked our wild wish to recall her again ;
For the voices of children, her darlings, her own,
Enchanted her soul with their rapturous tone,

While "daughter !" "wife !" "sister !" from loved ones again

Broke soft on her spirit in joyful refrain.

Her pilgrimage ended and heaven possessed,

We, alone, feel the pang, *she* has entered her Rest.

I HAVE learned a simple legend,
  Never found in books of lore,
Copied not from old tradition,
  Nor from classics read of yore;

But the breezes sang it to me
  With a low and soft refrain,
While the golden leaves and scarlet
  Fluttered down to catch the strain.

And the grand old trees above me,
  As their stately branches swayed,
Threw across my couch of crimson
  More of sunlight than of shade.

I had lain there dreaming, musing
  On the summer's vanished bloom,
Wondering if each penciled leaflet
  Did not mark some flow'ret's tomb;

Thinking how each tree could tell me
  Many a tale of warrior's fame; ·

Gazing at the sky, and asking
   How the "Indian Summer" came.

Then methought a whispered cadence
   Stole from out the haunted trees,
While the leaves kept dropping, dropping,
   To the music of the breeze.

"I will tell thee," said the whisper,
   "What I've learned from Nature's book;
For the sunbeams wrote this legend
   On the margin of a brook.

"'Tis about an Indian maiden,
   She the star-flower of her race,
With a heart whose soft emotions
   Rippled through her soul-lit face.

"All her tribe did homage to her,
   For her father was their chief;
He was stern, and she forgiving,—
   He brought pain, and she relief.

"And they called him 'Indian Winter,'
   All his actions were so cold;
Her they named the 'Indian Summer,'
   For she seemed a thread of gold

" Flashing through her native forest,
    Beaming in the wigwam lone,
Singing to the birds, her playmates,
    Till they warbled back her tone.

" When the summer days were ended,
    And the chilling months drew near,
When the clouds hung, dull and leaden,
    And the leaves fell, brown and sere,

" Brought they to the chieftain's presence
    One, a ' pale-face,' young and brave,
But whom youth nor manly valor
    Could from savage vengeance save.

" ' Bring him forth !' in tones of thunder
    Thus the ' Indian Winter' cried,
While the gentle ' Indian Summer'
    Softly flitted to his side.

" When the tomahawk was lifted,
    And the scalping-knife gleamed high,
Pride, revenge, and bloody hatred
    Glared within the warrior's eye ;

" And the frown upon his forehead
    Darker, deeper, sterner grew ;

While the lowering clouds above them
  Hid the face of heaven from view.

" 'Spare him ! oh, my father, spare him !'
  Friend and foe were thrust apart,
While the golden thread of sunlight
  Twined around the red man's heart.

" And her eye was full of pity,
  And her voice was full of love,
As she told him of the wigwam
  On the hunting-ground above,

" Where great Manito was talking,—
  She could hear him in the breeze ;
How he called the 'pale-face' brother—
  Smoked with him the pipe of peace.

" Then the warrior's heart relented,
  And the glittering weapon fell:
' For the maiden's sake,' he muttered,
  ' Thou art pardoned,—fare thee well !'

" And the sun, that would have slumbered
  'Till the spring-time came again,
Earthward from his garnered brightness
  Threw a flood of golden rain ;

"And the 'Indian Summer' saw it,
　She, the gentle forest child;
And to 'Indian Winter' whispered,
　'See how Manito has smiled!'

"All the tribe received the omen,
　And they called it by her name:
INDIAN SUMMER, INDIAN SUMMER,
　It will ever be the same.

"Though the 'pale-face' gave another
　To the lovely maid he won,
Nature still receives her tribute
　From the wigwam of the sun.

"Here, alone, this shining symbol
　Gilds the streamlet, warms the sod,
For no INDIAN SUMMER cometh
　Save where Indian feet have trod."

THE CHILDREN.

You may talk of the exquisite paintings
   You guard with the tenderest care;
Of your statues of Parian marble,
   So faultless, so perfect, so rare;
But give me a call, and I'll show you
   Some pictures more fair to behold
Than ever were drawn by the masters,
   Whose names down the ages have rolled.

At Christmas I took down my statues,
   My Cupids and Psyches and all;
And the gloom of the place made me shudder
   As I turned to the desolate wall.
Bright curls that the sunlight had garnished,
   Dark tresses the midnight had bound,
And mirth-loving eyes, all had vanished,
   While red lips could nowhere be found.

But now they are back in their niches,
   My statues of value untold:
My pictures in ebony framings,
   And some set in amber and gold.

27

The room has grown bright with their presence,
　The gloom and the silence have fled,
For the crown of His sweet benediction
　Still rests on each innocent head.

And the thought, as they gather each morning
　And murmur the prayer that He gave,
That His dear, loving arms are around them,
　Makes my own sinking heart, ofttimes, brave.
So I nestle down closely beside them,
　And trust, when the Saviour shall see
The white souls that flutter about me,
　His blessing will touch even me.

Am I faithful, I wonder, in tilling
　The soil of their hearts day by day?
Will the seed I am patiently sowing
　Spring up but to wither away?
The mold is not rocky nor barren,
　But tares may spring up—tares of sin ;
Yet I trust to His care all their future,
　Who gathers the golden sheaves in.

BABY MARGIE.

Came she with the April dawning;
  Such a tiny, tender thing,
Little sisters thought a seraph
  Bore her earthward 'neath its wing.
And they said her harp was heavy
  As her golden, starry crown,
Else the kind bestowing angel
  Would have tried to bring it down.

And they spoke in softest whispers
  When she nestléd to my breast,
Saying, as they gazed above them,
  " 'Twas so far she needeth rest."
So she slumbered, Baby Margie,
  Dreaming of her native skies;
This we knew, for, on awaking,
  Heaven still lingered in her eyes.

April flow'ret! Spring's first blossom!
  How our thoughts would onward rove,
Picturing, from her fair unfolding,
  What the perfect flower might prove!

Thinking how new joy would thrill us,
　　Deeper transports still be stirred,
When her trembling voice came freighted
　　With the first sweet, lisping word.

Musing how her step uncertain
　　Soon our guidance would repay;
Tender feet! Life's paths were rugged,—
　　All too rough to lure her stay.
So she wandered, Baby Margie,
　　Upward to the golden strand,—
Left the hearts that could not hold her,
　　Reaching toward the spirit-land.

Earth seems lone and drear without her,
　　Home is robbed of half its bliss,
For our hearts' exultant morning
　　Broke with her awakening kiss.
Faith looks up, but Love still turneth,
　　Bruised and bleeding, to the dust;
And, in tones of wildest anguish,
　　Cries to Him for perfect trust.

Lips whose gentlest pressure thrilled us,
　　Cheek and brow so saintly white,

Underneath the church-yard daisies
　　They have hid ye all from sight.
Though we yielded back her spirit
　　Trustingly to God who gave,
'Twas as if our hearts were buried
　　When we left our darling's grave.

There's an empty crib beside us,
　　And the wrappings still remain,
Showing, from their careful folding,
　　Where a precious form has lain.
Yestereve a string of coral,
　　In my searching, met my view,
And a half-worn, crimson stocking
　　Prisoned in a dainty shoe.

When the children's sports are over,
　　When their mimic work is done,
When they come and kneel before me,
　　Hushed and solemn, one by one,—
When their low-voiced "Our Father"
　　Meekly from their young lips fall,
And they rise and wait in silence,
　　Then I miss her most of all.

'Twas her lips, while yet she lingered,
　　Claimed the last, the warmest kiss,

And their saddened, wistful glances
 Tell me truly what they miss.
And they wonder if she wants me
 In her home so strange and new ;
'Tis a point I cannot answer,
 For I often wonder, too.

Though I know the seraphs bore her
 To the mansions of the blest ;
Still, I think, she must have missed me
 When she left my longing breast.
And I trust some angel-mother,
 Followed by her pleading eyes,
Took her gently to her bosom
 When my cherub reached the skies.

Father-love, I know, is holy :
 In the heavenly Parent's arms
All His spotless lambs are gathered,
 Free from pain or earth's alarms.
But the thought that some fond mother,
 Yearning for her babe below,
Clasped my little orphan-angel
 To her heart, with love aglow,
Makes me feel that naught is wanting
 To perfect her bliss above ;

For her gentle, trusting spirit
   Needs a mother's tenderest love.

Kind Old Year! thou gavest our treasure
   With the opening buds of spring,
And our grateful spirits thanked thee
   For thy vernal offering.
But, alas! thou couldst not leave her
   To the chance of coming woe,
So thou blessed her dreamless slumber
   Ere thy summons came to go.

Fond Old Year! Such tearful memories
   Bind my mourning soul to thee!
In thy arms my baby tasted
   Life and immortality.
Thou and she have gone together,—
   Crossed the bounds of Time's dark swell,—
Therefore let my benediction
   Mingle with thy parting knell.

B*

TO A NIGHT-BLOOMING CEREUS.

BEAUTIFUL flower, with petals white,
That only blooms in the hush of night,
That never reveals to the sunlight bold
The inner beauty thy petals hold,
As I sit to night, keeeping watch o'er thee,
Thou seem'st to blossom alone for me.

I have known some hearts like thine own, fair one,
That never would ope to the glaring sun ;
Whose wealth of sweetness was treasured up
Like the golden threads in thy opening cup ;
Who had never a throb nor a glow at all,
Except for the heart that received them all.

And some hearts I have known that the gathering
    gloom
Has seemed to call into perfect bloom ;
Whose garnered brightness with magic power
Came blossoming out in life's darkest hour ;

34

Who waited, like thee and the stars on high,
Ere they gave their splendor to earth and sky.

Beautiful flower, in thy robe of white,
Thou seem'st like an angel of peace to-night ;
But, like joys that have vanished, or fond hopes dead,
Thy wondrous beauty will all have fled
When I wake at morn, and I'll only see
The corpse of the flower that bloomed for me.

But, like other memories I treasure there,
And hide in my heart with a miser's care,
In that inner temple, that none may see
Except when I lift the veil for thee,
I will hold the thought of our converse sweet,
With hope and rapturous joy replete.

For we've talked together, thou and I,
When none but God and ourselves was nigh ;
I have touched my cheek to thy snowy tips,
And breathed a prayer on thy opening lips ;
And thou, in turn, to my weary heart
Didst strength and comfort and faith impart.

And now I will bid thee a fond "good-night,"
With thy petals spread as for upward flight ;

And my thoughts shall be of an angel flower
That blooms above in a fairer bower,
Where the dear ones, waiting, may turn to see
The beautiful bud that unclosed for me.

THE ELDER BROTHER.

AFFECTIONATELY DEDICATED TO DR. JOSEPH A. SMITH, OF
FORT MADISON, IOWA.

THERE are heroes in war, there are heroes in story,
   Whose courage, undaunted when leaden rain fell,
Has covered their names with an unfading glory,
   Whose fullness the dim, distant ages will tell.
But the theme of my song went not forth with the rattle
   Of steel-bristling bayonet, bugle and drum,
But stood on the ramparts of life's changeful battle
   As sentinel, guarding the bulwarks of Home.

They are graven in blood upon history's pages,
   The names of those martyrs who hallowed our sod;
But heroes like mine pass unsung through the Ages
   To fill the first ranks at the roll-call of God.
There are laurels awaiting the conqueror leaving
   The red field of carnage where triumph was given,
But none see the garlands the angels are weaving
   For him whose *grand deeds* are his bay-wreath in
      heaven.

O mariner ! you whom the waves have swept over
  And scooped from your heart its glad sunlight and
    bloom,
When the blackness of darkness around seemed to hover,
  And yawning beneath was a fathomless tomb,
Wast succored, like me, from Despair's ruthless ocean,
  Whose billows of Doubt left nor compass nor guide?
Wast shielded, sustained, by a brother's devotion,
  Whose love was the life-boat that weathered the
    tide?

Or when, 'mid earth's trials, the night gathered o'er
    you,
  And, strength and heart failing, weak flesh could not
    stand,
Still constant and true did a light gleam before you,
  Held o'er the rough paths by a brother's firm hand?
If so, you can measure the depth of my feeling
  For one whose devotion has never grown dim,
Nor chide the wild impulse that often comes stealing,
  When gratitude prompts, to do homage to him.

It was not a father, a sister, a mother,
  That made intercession that Mercy might win ;
Our pardon was sealed by a dear "elder brother,"
  Who gave His own life as a ransom for sin.

With earth-love, earth-memories clinging around it,
   This name to our great Mediator was given
To show the sweet tie of affection that bound it
   To Him who still pleads our forgiveness in heaven.

MADELINE BOWER.

She perished in beauty,
  As withers a rose
When its delicate petals
  Begin to unclose.
She passed from among us,
  And left us to pine
For the treasure we could not
  With calmness resign.
The light of our home
  Has grown dim since the hour
It lost the dear presence
  Of Madeline Bower.

Her voice was like music
  That trembles along,
When the last strain is sung
  Of a soul-thrilling song.
So witchingly mellow,
  You'd stand by her side,
And drink in its echo
  Long after it died.

Now vainly we list
  At the still, twilight hour
For the notes of our song-bird—
  Lost Madeline Bower.

Her tresses of light
  Seemed o'er marble to flow,
For her brow could have rivaled
  The purest of snow.
Ah! none but bereaved ones,
  Who've wept o'er the clay,
Can know of our pangs
  When 'twas hidden away.
One tress from its sisters
  Was severed that hour:
'Twas all we might claim
  Of sweet Madeline Bower.

Oh, would they could waft us—
  Our treasures above—
Some tender remembrance,
  Some token of love,—
A mystical sign
  That they do not forget;
A blessed assurance
  They yearn for us yet!

4*

Or is it designed
  That we hear not nor see
One trace of our loved ones
  Till death sets us free?
Do we pass through the vale,
  With its shadow and blight,
That the glory of heaven
  May burst on our sight?
If so, how ecstatic,
  How rapturous the hour
Our freed souls are welcomed
  By Madeline Bower!

HOLD THE LIGHT.

Ho ! thou traveler on life's highway,
  Moving carelessly along ;
Pausing not to note the darkness
  Lowering o'er the struggling throng ;
Waiting not to mark how feebly
  Some are laboring in the fight,
Bending on thee wistful glances,—
  Turn aside, and hold the light !

Look ! upon thy right a brother
  Wanders blindly from the way ;
And upon thy left a sister,
  Frail and erring, turns astray.
One kind word, perchance, may save them,
  Guide their wayward steps aright ;
Canst thou, then, withhold thy counsel ?
  No ! but fly, and hold the light !

Hark ! a feeble wail of anguish
  Bursts from the advancing throng,

And a little child is groping
   Through the shadows deep and long.
'Tis a timid orphan, sinking
   'Neath misfortune's withering blight;
Friends, home, love, are all denied her:
   Oh, in pity hold the light!

Not alone in heathen darkness,
   Where the pagan bows the knee,
Worshiping his senseless image
   With a blind idolatry,—
Where no blessed gospel teachings
   E'er illume the soul's dark night,
Comes the cry to listless mortals,
   Wild and pleading, "Hold the light!"

Here as well, in life's broad highway,
   Are benighted wanderers found;
And if all the strong would aid them,
   Lights would glimmer all around.
Acts of love and deeds of kindness
   Then would make our pathway bright,
And we'd have no need of calling,
   "Ho! thou traveler, hold the light!"

A TEMPERANCE POEM.

INSCRIBED TO THE LADIES.

Mr. Lionel Lightfoot, a man, you must know,
  Whose life had been upright and blameless,
To the capital's chamber came three years ago
  From a county that here shall be nameless.
He was loyal at heart, but all tyranny spurned,
  And, when comrades endeavored to prove him,
Allegiance to Alcohol's power he spurned,—
  Neither jeers nor persuasions could move him.
Though at club-room or bar they would oftentimes meet,
  He ne'er treated, nor could be entreated to treat.

And now 'twas mid-winter,—the question was up
To legally sanction or banish the cup.
The ladies had come, with their beauty and grace,
To cheer the desponding and brighten the place.
Discussions grew warm, but all pleading was vain,
For Alcohol triumphed, and Whisky again

Would desolate hearthstones,—bring Want and Despair
To dear ones once guarded with tenderest care.

And Lightfoot lamented,—his mother's calm smile
Seemed resting upon him,—her voice, too, the while,
Those soft, tender tones to remembrance so dear,
Sweet, earnest, and true, floated back to his ear :
" My son, if they sanction this blight of the soul,
Forget not my teachings—beware of the bowl !"

The day had departed, the twilight had fled,
At the still hour of midnight the Old Year lay dead.
The breeze sighed its requiem, the ocean its moan,
For the aged and mighty who perished alone ;
But the sun of the morning rose fair o'er the scene
Where, in night's fearful silence, the death-pall had been.

And now it was New Year,—"a happy New Year,"—
    And young Lightfoot were guilty of treason
If he failed to the fair ones in person to pay
    His dues, with the dues of the season.
So, calling on Fairface, an exquisite dandy,
An ardent believer in spirits—of brandy,
He found him perturbed—in a *barbarous* passion,—
His moustache had been trimmed quite too close for the
        fashion ;

His head, too—oh, shocking to add to the list !—
Two hairs on the left the Macassar had missed.

But Lightfoot restored him : " The former," he said,
" Looked so foreign—*distangué*——"(a beautiful red
He fain would have added, but paused, lest the ire
Of his comrade might set his adornment on fire.)
Then, waiting till Fairface made smooth as a die
For the fiftieth time his "miwaculous tie,"
With assurance his collar just touched his goatee
Without varying, in distance, the slightest degree,
With cane between gloves of invisible green,
They called on Miss Mabel—society's queen ;
And, listening the while to the lively narrations
Of her numerous calls and her morning libations,
" *Your* health !" cries ma belle ; returns Lightfoot, " Ex-
         cuse me,
I never indulge." " What ! on New Year's refuse *me !*
Politeness demands it ; beside" (soft and low),
" Champagne is so perfectly harmless, you know."

Ah, woman, fair temptress, thou knew'st not the while
The doom that was sealed by that innocent smile ;
Or how fatal the spell in that voice, that was given
To lure man from vice and direct him to heaven.

Thou saw'st not the phantoms that clutched at the bowl,
Nor the serpents that fastened their fangs in his soul ;
Thou heardst not the clank of the chains that were wound
By fiends that kept mocking the spirit they bound.

So Lightfoot was tempted, and yielded at last,
   Beguiled by this siren of beauty ;
And, quitting her presence, he carried away
   Her smile of approval as booty.
A dangerous trophy, these smiles of the fair ;
They melted his good resolutions to air ;
For though he had reasoned, "I'll only partake
This once of the wine, for the fair charmer's sake,"
He was sadly mistaken,—the breach had been made,
The fortress surrendered, its inmates betrayed ;
The noble resolves that had guarded the tower
Where Faith held her torch in temptation's dark hour,
The purposes high that had stamped on his brow
The glory of manhood, oh, where were they now?

But why follow on with the twain as they flit
   From bower to bower, partaking?
Or tell how the feeble resolves of the one
   Were seized with an ague of shaking?
How, long before night-fall, he fancied his brain
Was dancing a reel on a circular plain?

How houses inverted, in warlike array,
Wheeled backward and forth in an endless *chassé* ?
We pass these sad pictures, nor linger to tell
How, step after step, from true manhood he fell.
How at first he took naught but the choicest of wine,—
Some ancient Madeira, or rum superfine ;
How he drank but with gentlemen, such as would deign
To touch no cheap brandy nor third-rate champagne.

Behold him, at last, in some vice-crowded den,
Where skulk the crouched forms of what once ranked as
      men ;
Where the pestilent fumes from each whisky-scorched
      throat
The pure air of heaven with plague-spots have smote ;
Where Malice, Pollution, and Wretchedness teem,
And Guilt stalks among them to mock and blaspheme.
There see him, the victim of Woman's soft smile,
Debauched and corrupted, degraded and vile.

Years pass, and again with our "pillars of State"
Is the same question pending in earnest debate ;
The fair ones are listeners ; Miss Mabel has come
To hear of the darkness in many a home,—
Of the desolate hearthstones the rum-fiend has made,
Of promises broken and loved ones betrayed.

She listens—grows weary—departing, at last,
She hastes to her chamber to think of the Past.
Though languid, she wooes a calm slumber in vain,
For the sleep that should soothe her but frenzies her brain.

She dreams—'tis of Lightfoot: she tempts him to drink.
He quaffs at her bidding, then ceases to shrink
From frequent indulgence of evils the worst;
His hopes are all blasted, his life is accurst;
She sees him descending from honor—renown—
And sinking to ruin—down—hopelessly down.
There, wrestling with rum-fiends, in fury he raves,
Like a soul reft of reason, on life's maddening waves.
Half palsied with fright, 'mid the demons he stands,
And wards off their blows with his skeleton hands.
His eyes start with horror, and fearfully gloat
On blades, newly whetted, that point at his throat.
He shudders and cringes from serpents that hiss
And dart their forked tongues from their slimy abyss;
And, reeling from terror, he howls in his pains,
As devils incarnate stand welding his chains;
While one, a pale imp, the grim valet of Death,
With fagots of sulphur is firing his breath.
O horror! it blazes! it seethes to his brain!
His heart-strings have cracked—the blood boils in each
     vein!

A shudder—a gasp—a wild effort to speak—
And Miss Mabel awakes with a hideous shriek.

O ladies! dear ladies! when next round the wine
Your delicate fingers caressingly twine,
When, like a soft blessing, the breath of your lips
Floats over and hallows the juice ere he sips,
Just call the crouched form of poor Lightfoot to view,
And know that the dream of Miss Mabel *was true.*
Then, by your allurements, teach man to refrain,
And prove that your charms were bestowed not in vain;
Let your spotless example illustrate the plan
That woman was made as a help-*meet* for man,
To warn him from treading the pathway of sin
By the beautiful love-light that glows from within.

And, oh! as ye muse on that Eden above,
Whence spirits departed are gazing in love,
And guarding their kindred, who, chained by the clay,
Are prone by the tempter to wander astray,
A father's fond blessing may greet you, the while,
A sister bend over your couch with a smile,
A mother, in accents of rapturous joy,
May sing how your warnings have rescued her boy.

Then woman, O woman! thy mission fulfill!
Know man is the subject—the slave to thy will!

Thou wast given to guide him,—his beacon and star
To cheer when beside him and gleam from afar.
Then *keep thy soul white,* for one shadow of sin
May dim the bright taper that burneth within ;
And vain are his struggles life's billows above,
When the beacon goes out in the light-house of love.

IN MEMORIAM.

WILLIAM G., ELDEST SON OF W. W. BELKNAP, SECRETARY
OF WAR.

TOUCH the harp with gentlest finger, let a strain of tenderest feeling
Pulsate through its flowing numbers, all its sweetest
chords revealing.
Let the tone be low and trembling, as if seraphs
hovered nigh;
Music such as floods the portal of the clime we call immortal:
Such as soothed his deathless spirit when he closed his
weary eye.

At the dawning—in the morning—in the sunrise of his
being,
Ere his step had lost its lightness or his eye grew dull of
seeing,
Ere his sunny brow was shadowed by earth's sorrow
or its gloom,

Ere a score of years had crowned him, thus the silent
    Reaper found him,
  Like a golden bud of promise, blighted in its early
    bloom.

It was meet that loving faces should, in silence, gather
    near him,
And that kindred hearts should murmur blessings as they
    strove to cheer him;
  Yet their yearnings could not hold him; all their
    pleading cries were vain;
And the blinding tears kept starting at the sacred hour
    of parting,
  For this cherished household treasure that no longer
    might remain.

And the father, bowed and stricken,—ah! his woe was
    past repeating
When the hand he pressed so fondly gave no more an
    answering greeting;
  When no loving voice came trembling from the cold
    lips white and dumb.
May he bow in true submission, musing on the clime
    elysian,
  Where the angel watcher whispers down the shining
    pathway, "Come!"

May the grass grow green above him, resting on his lowly
  pillow,
And in quiet sadness o'er him, bend the constant, pitying
  willow!
  May soft zephyrs sing low dirges as they pass his
    narrow bed!
May the gently-falling showers, as they kiss the drooping
  flowers,
Bid them bloom and shed fresh fragrance on the turf
  above his head!

JOSEY'S BIRTHDAY.

" MAMMA, tell me 'bout Good Friday,"
   Lisped the prattler at my knee,
With his sparkling eyes uplifted,
   Laughing in his roguish glee.

" Is't a pretty story, mamma?
   Won't you tell it right away?
Take me up, I want to hear it,
   Then I'll run along and play."

But I could not tell the story
   As the solemn dirges fell,
Tolling through the day that darkened
   With the crucifixion knell,—

Could not tell him how Redemption
   By a boundless love was won,
And a grand Atonement proffered
   Through a well-beloved Son!

So I said, with arms around him,
   " Yes, 'tis good, for you must know
That a little blue-eyed baby
   Came to me four years ago.

" Just four years to-day, my darling,
   Since you oped your wondering eyes,
'Mid the solemn hush that Nature
   Keeps for our great Sacrifice.

" Oh, the memories that clustered
   As that hallowed day wore on !
Little heads my breast had pillowed,—
   Little dimpled arms had gone.

" Little feet, that ran to meet me,
   Lying still and white and cold ;
Little eyes, that watched my coming,
   Hid beneath the church-yard mold !

" Then when vesper-hymns outfloating
   Told the day was well-nigh spent,
' Only Son,' the singers chanted,
   And my heart responded, Lent.

c*

" Was it but the distant shadow
    Of His sufferings—of His Cross—
Made me fold my baby closer,
    Shuddering at my fancied loss?

" Who can tell?   The Father knoweth:
    Lent, not given, are all that come ;
When 'tis best that they should leave us,
    He will gently call them home.

" But, my pet, you have not listened !
    Mamma's boy is off at play !
Thread of sunlight, gleaming, flashing,
    Through this sacred, Hallowed Day."

A WELCOME TO OUR "JO."

(MISS KATE PERRY, OF KEOKUK, IOWA.)

A WELCOME back to her who went
   Abroad for her own pleasure,
Yet generously sent her friends
   An overflowing measure!
We grasp her hand with right good will, ·
   While memory fondly lingers
Upon the pictures sketched for "home"
   By these same busy fingers.

The Rhine, in all its winding course,
   Ne'er met a happier rover,
Nor Drusus, in his youthful prime,
   A more adoring lover.
And this is why the rippling waves
   In murmurs seemed to bless her,
While Drusus reached his shadowy arms,
   ·Imploring, to caress her.

I wonder, on those moonlit nights,
   When sky and stream were golden,

As she, a listener, heard entranced,
  Some legend tender—olden,—
If her own voice went floating out
  With all its wondrous power,
Awaking many an echoing tone
  At that entrancing hour !

Did siren with the golden hair,
  On distant heights appearing,
Still her soft notes of deep despair
  And give attentive hearing ?
Did voyagers on passing barks,
  Approaching late and early,
Drink in the sweet, bewildering strains
  Of our own matchless Loreley ?

The prayer went up for heavenly care
  Through storm and wave to bring her,
For scores of hearts have learned to love
  Our sweet impassioned singer.
Her life has proved, in war and peace,
  For dear ones fondly caring,
"The bravest are the tenderest,
  The loving are the daring."

Friends, read to her the parable
  (She's read it oft unbidden)

Of talents graciously bestowed,—
  Of one, too, that was hidden.
If "good and faithful" she would prove,
  Let not her gifts lie sleeping;
Let Voice and Pen improve the trust
  Confided to her keeping.

6

A DIRGE FOR HORACE GREELEY.

WEEP, weep, O my country! the cord has been severed
  That bound the great heart of a statesman to thee;
The spirit has fled that so nobly endeavored
  To save from Disunion the land of the Free.
The beautiful rod and the strong staff are broken,
  A gem from the casket of glory is reft;
He is gone, but his eloquent words as a token
  Of genius unrivaled shall ever be left.

'Mid the storms of the past, though the billows swept
      o'er him,
  He stood, all undaunted by tempest or tide;
For the Nation, his idol, lay bleeding before him,
  And he sprang to his duty and knelt by her side.
The Union, the home of the brave and true-hearted,
  Half palsied through fear by War's startling command,
With white arms upraised, all her courage departed,
  In silent despair gave the statesman her hand.

As tender as brave, with a patriot's devotion,
  He held and sustained her till danger was past;

With whispers of cheer checked the rising commotion,
   And led her, unharmed, to a haven at last.
And when the fierce roar of the battle was over,
   And Peace brooded down over hill-side and plain,
He gathered the bands we thought scattered forever,
   And tried, with firm hand, to unite them again.

The boon of a Nation we claimed as his dower,—
   Of her he had struggled so nobly to save;
But friends turned aside at the hope-freighted hour,
   And freemen bestowed on their Greeley—a grave.
Yet it was not defeat,—he, unmurmuring, bore it,
   Till stung by the venom of taunting and sneer;
Then shrank his great heart from the clutches that tore it,
   While mind fell a victim to torturing fear.

Ah, friends! ye should learn that all brave hearts are
       tender;
   That heroes stand firm 'mid the clash of the sword;
But spirits like his may be forced to surrender
   When the weapon ye use is a low, scathing word.
I tell you 'twere kinder if blood had flowed freely,
   Had our martyr been slain by an enemy's hand,
Than to sting him to madness,—to offer our Greeley
   A sacrifice here, in his own native land!

Yet worth cannot die; and, on history's pages,
   His record will tell what he dared for our sake;
And proudly reveal to the oncoming ages
   How a statesman can live and a *true heart can break.*
Oh, that generous heart! it was full to o'erflowing
   When the wife of his youth and his country were there;
But the one had passed on, and the other was going
   Far, far from his reach, and he *died of despair.*

LAKE MICHIGAN.

WRITTEN DURING THE JUBILEE AT CHICAGO.

WHILE thousands throng each crowded mart,
   And gaze around in mute surprise,
I turn with an adoring heart
   To thee, fair mirror of the skies.
Yet not in silence can I pour
   My full heart out, fair Lake, to thee,
So, humbly kneeling on thy shore,
   I chant thy praise, *my* Jubilee.

The purple clouds are all drawn back
   From heaven's blue vault, that I may trace
Its distant verge,—its shining track
   Held to thy heart in close embrace.
The roseate flush that tinged the sky
   Has slowly turned to burnished gold,
And every wave that hurries by
   Clasps all of sunlight it can hold.

I saw thee not, Lake Michigan,
   When all aglow—a sheet of flame ;

When forth the frenzied people ran
　　To shriek for help—to call thy name.
Chicago, thine own cherished bride,
　　Thou mightst not succor—couldst not save ;
But fettered lay as flames spread wide
　　And scooped for her a yawning grave.

The loss was ours ; we mourned with thee
　　That she should fall,—a nation mourned ;
Nor deemed we then we e'er should see
　　Her hopes restored, her strength returned.
" Forever lost, forever gone !"
　　Came through thy murmuring wavelets' swell ;
" Forever lost, forever gone !"
　　We echoed back,—her funeral knell.

Yet now, so soon, a wondering throng
　　Crowd to thy shore in hushed surprise,
And there behold (grand theme for song)
　　Chicago, Phœnix-like, arise.
A world lamented when she fell,
　　And now, 'neath turret, tower, and dome,
A multitude of voices tell
　　Her year of Jubilee has come.

Chicago, City of the Lake,
　　Bride of this lovely inland sea,

Thy resurrection-glories wake
   A dream of what thou yet shalt be.
Undaunted in thy darkest hour,
   Thyself hast brought the awakening dawn;
Thy energy has been the power
   That led, and still shall lead thee on.

THE SHADOWS ON THE WALL.

Fever sapped my very life-blood, frenzy fired my tortured
  brain,
And the friends who watched beside me, felt their lingering hopes were vain.
I was going—going from them, all unconscious of their
  fears;
Hastening to the Silent Valley, deaf to moans and blind
  to tears.
But a change was wrought at midnight—the destroyer's
  hand was stayed,
And the frenzy and the fever fled, affrighted and dis-
  mayed.
And the dear ones who had trembled as I neared the
  mystic goal,
Spoke in glad, rejoicing whispers as light slumber held
  control;
All, save one, the youngest—fairest—gentle friend of
  other years,
Who knelt reverently beside me, and returned her thanks
  with tears.

Since the sunny days of childhood we had known each
    other well,
And each fleeting year we numbered but increased love's
    magic spell ;
But, till sickness felled me, never did her acts of love
    divine
Seem to drop, like gems unnumbered, from a great ex-
    haustless mine.
With a sister's sweet devotion would her young head o'er
    me bow,
As she bathed my cheeks with kisses, and with tear-drops
    dewed my brow,
Like a fond and gentle mother on her bosom lay my
    head, .
And, in soft, endearing accents, speak of happy hours
    long fled.

When the dreadful dream was ended, when delirium's
    spell was broke,
When, with all an infant's weakness, I to consciousness
    awoke,
I could see the form of Emma round my darkened cham-
    ber glide,
And could hear her sweet voice breathing soothing whis-
    pers by my side.

Not till stars were shining brightly in the blue sky over-
    head

Would she leave me to my slumbers with a Sibyl's noise-
    less tread,

Then, within the room adjoining, sat she with attentive
    ear,

Ready, at the slightest murmur, at my bedside to ap-
    pear.

Well, one eve my eye had wandered from the bright and
    cheerful light

That came streaming through the doorway, to the wall so
    smooth and white,

When methought I heard a footfall ('twas not Emma's, I
    was sure)

Stepping lightly through the hall and pausing at the inner
    door.

It was opened—oh, so softly I could scarcely hear the
    sound ;

Had a human hand unclosed it, or were spirits stalking
    round ?

While I looked and thought and wondered, lo! there
    glided from the hall,

With a stealthy tread, a shadow, and stood waiting on
    the wall.

"Twas as handsome as the "photos" done by Emerson
    last week;
Its two lips were slightly parted, as though just about to
    speak;
And its eyes—I lost their color with their most bewitch-
    ing flash,
Yet I saw it sported whiskers and a slightly-curled mous-
    tache;
Then its nose was sharp and classic,—it was finely built
    and tall,
And a full round chin and forehead had this shadow on
    the wall.

Quick before my wondering vision did a second shadow
    glide;
It excelled the air in fleetness till it reached the other's
    side.
Ah! full well that face, that figure, and those graceful
    curls were known,
For, with sportive pencil, oft had I the self-same outline
    drawn.
And, so great was my amazement, I my voice could scarce
    suppress
When I saw these phantom figures meeting with a warm
    caress;

And—my memory here grows faithless—I can only just
    recall
That I saw four lips of shadow meet upon the pictured
    wall.

When the pantomime was ended, I grew restless from sur-
    prise,
And, remembering not my weakness, I in vain essayed
    to rise ;
But the shadows heard my movement, and they fled before
    my gaze
With the swiftness of the lightning, choosing wisely
    different ways ;
And when, in a moment after, bent a fair face o'er my
    bed,
Eyes were closed and breast was heaving: "Sleeping
    sweetly," Emma said ;
Never dreamed she that the sleeper had been witness to
    it all,
Or, more truly, to the tableau of the shadows on the wall.

Often have I seen the *substance* of the shadow first since
    then,
And no nobler heart is numbered in the family of men.

He is worthy of his Emma, who, now standing by his
    side,
Does not note his beaming glance of mingled tenderness
    and pride.
With one hand upon his shoulder and·the other clasped
    in mine,
She's been coaxing for a poem about " Charles and Em-
    meline;"
And I've quickly snatched my pencil for the first time to
    recall
To the twain the summer's eve I saw the shadows on the
    wall.

LINES

AFFECTIONATELY INSCRIBED TO MY FATHER'S FRIEND, HON.
D. F. MILLER.

DEAR friend, 'twas not thy word of praise,
Bestowed upon my simple lays,
That woke, as if by magic art,
A thrill responsive in my heart.
'Twas the fond mention of a word
That all my tenderest feelings stirred,—
A name the Past endeared to thee,
And fraught with love and trust to me.

His step, his touch, his vanished tone
Seem mingling often with thine own.
The teacher, as in days of yore,
Repeats his sage instructions o'er ;
The pupil, in the flush of youth,
Lists to those golden words of truth,
And dreams such dreams as manhood may
When proud ambition points his way.

74

Ah! neither then had locks of white!
He, on life's grand meridian height,
Thou, with thy powers as yet untried,
And I a prattler at thy side.
It seems so strange to see thee now
With frosts of age upon thy brow,
Yet sweet to know thy love for him
Has never faltered nor grown dim.

How much they gain of heavenly lore,
Our loved and lost who "go before"!
The jasper walls will brighter glow
When from them lean the forms we know.
Our foretaste of celestial bliss
Will be a welcoming clasp and kiss;
Our recompense for every pain
Will be this "gathering home" again.

And wilt thou not hold converse sweet
Where constant friends their vows repeat?
Where change can mar, nor time can dim,
Wilt thou not learn again of him?
With the deep mystery of the skies
Unveiled before thy wondering eyes,
What guide more meet, if choice be given,
To lead thee to the highest heaven?

WHAT ARE THE SNOW-FLAKES?

SAY, whence come the snow-flakes—the pure, fleecy snow-
    flakes,
  That flutter so softly, so tremblingly by?
Are they foam from the ocean of ether above us,
  Or petals from roses that blow in the sky?
Do seraphs who wander beside the still waters,
  Or linger, entranced, in fair bowers above,
Keep culling the leaves of the blossoms around them
  To scatter them earthward as tokens of love?

Are they down, that the beautiful Angel of Summer,
  At parting, so noiselessly shakes from her wings?
Or heralds sent forth by the glittering Frost-King
  To tell of the jewels he lavishly brings?
Oh! I sometimes half dream, as I watch the flakes falling,
  That 'tis Purity's self gliding down from the skies,
Till, meeting our earth-damps of sin and pollution,
  They melt her to tears and of pity she dies.

THE BABY.

ALL this blessed summer morning,
With the golden sunlight round me,
Has my heart bowed down, o'erburdened
    With its mournful tenderness,—
With this longing for the baby
That for weary months has bound me,
For the look her blue eyes gave me,
    And her winning, fond caress.

I have heard some grief is deeper:
That of mourning ones still yearning
For the brave hearts stilled forever
    'Mid the clash of war's alarms,
But I know no sadder picture
Than fond memory, slowly turning
From the past, to gaze in silence
    On a mother's empty arms.

Oh, they told me, those who knew not,
That I would not miss her ever,—
Would not always start expectant

At the mention of her name;
But as many moons have vanished
Since the Father bade us sever,
As her brief existence numbered,
    And the void seems just the same.

Often, as the night advanceth,
From my troubled sleep upstarting,
Am I roused by what seem echoes
    Of my baby's plaintive cry.
And I catch familiar accents
From my trembling lips departing,—
Whispers of some name endearing,
    Or some soothing lullaby.

And my spirit sinks when fadeth
This, my slumber's bright creating,
Till Faith breathes, " Her fleeting life
    Was but a glimpse of heaven to thee.
There in changeless, endless beauty
Is thy angel babe awaiting
To be folded to thy bosom
    Through a long eternity."

So I gaze off with the dawning,
To where day in light is breaking,—
Where the white gleam of the marble

Tells me some death's waves have crossed ;
And I muse, without a shudder,
On that sleep that hath no waking,
For I know it must o'ertake me
  Ere I see the loved and lost.

Oh, I trust they'll lay my ashes
Close beside this faded blossom !
Would my arms might twine around her,
  And her lips to mine be pressed !
'Twere so sweet to think the casket
Might be folded to my bosom,
That our dust might not be parted
  In that deep, unbroken rest !

OCTOBER.

Have you seen a gentle maiden
  Flitting down your forest aisles,
With her shining tresses flowing,
  And her red lips wreathed with smiles?
With the golden leaves of autumn
  Round her white brow lightly pressed,
And its modest crimson berries
  Blushing on her virgin breast?

Have you heard her breezy footfalls
  Trembling through the rustling grass?
Have you caught her mellow whispers
  To the song-birds as they pass?
Have you marked the wondrous brightness
  Beaming from her tender eye,
When the rippling streamlets murmured
  Blessings as she glided by?

Yes, you've seen her, fair October:
  Since she sought your forest aisles,

She has lightened hill and valley
   With the glory of her smiles.
She has crossed your babbling river,
   Lingered on your wild-flower track,
Until now the gates of cloud-land
   Softly ope to woo her back.

She has floated, floated upward,
   Over meadow, stream, and wood,
Till her golden hair is dabbled
   In the sunset's crimson blood.
She has breathed her latest blessing,
   She has wrought her parting spell ;
Waning autumn's benediction,—
   Sweet October, fare thee well !

D*

MY MOTHER'S FRIEND.

LOVINGLY INSCRIBED TO "GRANDMA FULTON."

You wondered why my fingers clasped
　So lovingly that withered hand ;
The tenderness that filled my heart
　You saw, yet could not understand.
Yet will the mystery be explained :
　My impulse you will comprehend
When you are told that aged one
　Was, in her youth, my mother's friend.

Those snowy locks in other years
　Luxuriant hung, in graceful curls
Perchance, and oft touched mother's cheek
　With soft caress, when both were girls.
That breath commingled with her own,
　As the young head would trusting bend,
To tell, in low, confiding tone,
　Her secrets to her early friend.

With such a bitter, aching void
　As life must hold when mothers go,

No matter when,—if full of years,
  Or in their noontide's golden glow,
It is not strange my weary heart
  Should long to feel those arms descend
And fold in motherly embrace
  The daughter of her early friend.

I wonder if the mists of years
  Melt in the radiance of the skies?
Will heaven restore our faded bloom,
  And youth return in Paradise?
Do blighted hopes and vanished joys
  Revive, return when earth's dreams end?
If so, what glad surprise awaits,
  Beyond the blue, my mother's friend!

Oh, peaceful be her closing hour,
  And soothing the familiar tone
That bids her deathless spirit rise
  Where weight of years is all unknown!
May the same hand that points her way
  Clasp mine when life and care shall end,
And bear me to the shining shore,
  To join my mother's early friend!

THEY SPOKE IN WHISPERS.

THEY spoke in whispers; it was not
　　Because a crowd was nigh,
For all alone they breathed each thought
　　Beneath a moonlit sky.
That stilly hour but nursed the flame
　　That o'er their spirits swept;
And Nature, hallowed by the same,
　　A sacred silence kept.

They spoke in whispers; was't because
　　They feared the birds might hear?
Or that the light-winged breeze might pause
　　And bend a listening ear?
Or that the sweet wild-flowers, which stood
　　So near, in listening crowds,
Might snatch their secret,—that the dew
　　Might tell it to the clouds?

Or did they fear the fair young moon
　　Might ope her silver bars,

To let the echo of each word
　　Glide upward to the stars?
Or that the ripples of the stream
　　That kissed that quiet shore
Might catch their vows, and to the waves
　　Repeat the story o'er?

Or did they dream the heavens would speak
　　Through countless starry eyes,
Bent downward on each love-lit cheek
　　In tremulous surprise?
I cannot tell, but only know
　　That earth and air and sky
Seemed conscious of the rapturous thrill
　　That marked each fond reply.

Soft grew their whispers; gently moved
　　Her crimson lips apart,
As if to drink the waves of love
　　That rippled from his heart.
Then nearer stole the envious breeze,
　　To share that whispered tone;
Too late—'twas hushed—their souls had learned
　　A language all their own.

ONLY LENT.

Morning's hush was all around me,
   Silence brooded everywhere,
When the early dawning found me
   Bowed and crushed by wild despair ;
For my eldest-born before me
   Prostrate lay with faltering breath,
And the shudder that stole o'er me
   Seemed the icy touch of death.
Then the solemn hush was broken,
   Tones from distant bells were blent.
When I asked, " What means this token ?"
   I was answered, " Only Lent."

Only Lent ! To fastings holy,
   Soon to end at Easter-tide,
They referred, while I bent lowly
   O'er the blossom at my side.
Tender plant, whose love had lighted
   Days of toil and nights of gloom ;
But whose buds of hope were blighted,
   Blighted in their early bloom.

Ten short years to bless and cheer me
   Had this April flower been sent ;
Ten short springs to blossom near me,
   Then to wither.   Only lent.

Heavier seemed my cross unto me
   Than before was ever borne,
When she whispered that she knew me
   As I wept that sacred morn.
I forgot Who once hung bleeding
   While this Day was wrapped in gloom ;
For our ransom interceding,
   Bearing thus the sinner's doom ;
And my soul cried out in sorrow
   For the deep affliction sent,
Murmuring, " He may claim to-morrow
   Her whose life is only lent."

But the morrow came and ended,
   And another dawned and sped ;
Then the morn when He ascended—
   Rose in triumph from the dead,
Crowned with resurrection glory;
   Gladly rang the matin bells,
Pealing forth the wondrous story
   Through our plains and woods and dells.

Then the sweet, pale face beside me
  Whiter grew by suffering spent;
Joy without, but hope denied me:
  She, I knew, was only lent.

Days since then I've sadly numbered;
  Twelve young moons have come and gone,
And her precious form has slumbered,—
  Cold and still has slumbered on.
But her deathless soul ascended
  To a loving Saviour's side,
Where, with angel voices blended,
  Hers will chant at Easter-tide.
When I know her joyous spirit,
  Resting thus in sweet content,
All heaven's transports may inherit,
  Should I grieve, though only lent?

Once again through tears I hearkened
  To the deep-toned bells that rang,
Heralding the day that darkened
  'Neath the crucifixion pang.
Then the angel of Bestowment,
  Pitying my lonely hours,
Bent above my couch a moment
  With a bud from Eden bowers;

As it touched my yearning bosom,
　　Life and hope and joy seemed sent
To enfold the tender blossom,
　　Given perhaps; perhaps but lent!

Last year's crucifixion morning
　　Held for me a heavy cross;
For 'twas then I heard the warning
　　Of my near approaching loss;
Now again its dawn is over,
　　Prayers and matins all are said,
And an angel seems to hover,
　　Breathing blessings on my head.
Hark! she whispers, "I am near thee;
　　Let not life in gloom be spent,
Let this blossom soothe and cheer thee;
　　Christ himself was only lent."

8*

ESTO PERPETUA.

DEDICATED TO THE STUDENTS OF THE COLLEGE OF PHY-
SICIANS AND SURGEONS, AT KEOKUK, IOWA, CLASSES OF
1875–76.

STUDENTS! as again ye gather
  Where your feet have trod before,
Ope your minds to Wisdom's teachings,
  Drink them in and thirst for more!
In your Alma Mater's shadow
  Sages, men of learning, wait,
Ready, with the keys of Science,
  To unlock her golden gate.

Those who dwell in mountain-passes,
  Narrowed in by rock and vale,
Strive, and serve an humble purpose,
  Make their *little lives* avail.
But, with prairies circling round you,
  Stretching beyond human ken,
And this grand old river near you,
  Need ye rank as common men?

Why, it seems such thoughts should thrill you
  As would leap their prison-bars,
Mounting, eagle-plumed, above you,
  Till they almost touched the stars !
Vastness, richness, boundless beauty
  Urge you up to loftiest height ;
Rouse you to prolonged endeavor,—
  Nerve you for Life's coming fight.

Be ye watchful, patient, gentle,
  Quick to soothe and strong to bear ;
For the healing of the nation
  Is confided to your care.
Let your tones be glad and hopeful
  If new life ye would impart ;
Let your cheering smiles of greeting
  Fall, like sunlight, on the heart.

Oh, be firm as rocks of granite
  When temptations bar your way !
Let not vice, with its allurements,
  Turn your steadfast steps astray.
Pure should be the man who waiteth
  Where a spirit's bonds are riven,
And the freed soul, angel-guided,
  Wings its way to home and heaven.

EDA.

AGED THIRTY-THREE YEARS.

ONE sweet, consoling thought comes to me as I write :
Her deathless spirit, snowy-winged, is nearer us to-night
That when it dwelt below, imprisoned by the clay,
Longing to join the yearning group that mourned its
     lengthened stay.

For heaven is not so far that loved ones may not find
The shadowed homes and longing hearts of those they
     left behind ;
They rest a little while by Eden's placid streams,
And then glide back, on noiseless wings, to soothe us in
     our dreams.

Not vanished from our sight,—no, no, not gone to stay !
Her touch—her smile—her gentle tone can never pass
     away ;
The twilight brings again a wealth of sunny hair,—
A brow of white, a hand, a voice that points and whispers,
     "There."

We know that she will wait, nor seek the furthest skies,
Until there is a gathering in of all earth's broken ties;
The eldest-born—the first to cross death's mystic tide,
And first to greet, with welcoming clasp, upon the other
      side.

Be our lives as pure, as free from stain or sin,
As the white soul that heard His call and softly floated
      in ;
And if 'tis ours to choose what recompense be given
For every pang, we only ask to share our darling's heaven.

MAMMA'S VALENTINE.

"MAMMA!" cried a roguish elf,
Snatching kisses for himself,
Standing, tiptoe, by my side
With a look of boyish pride,
"See how tall! If you'll be mine,
I will be *your* Valentine."

"Yes, my darling, so you may;
Whisper low what you would say;
Breathe it soft, in tenderest tone,
Vow to live for me alone;
Learn, in time, that love *in part*
Never holds a woman's heart."

"When I grow to be a man
Mayn't I love you all I can?
Is it silly, mamma, say,
When I kiss you this-a-way?
Ain't I yours, and ain't you mine?
And don't that mean Valentine?"

"Yes, my sweet,—you understand,—
Lip to lip, and hand in hand ;
Heart that wakes an answering thrill,
Soul to soul responsive still ;
All thine own, as thou art mine,
Dearest, truest, Valentine."

NELLY'S STORY.

It was on a lovely evening
  In the merry month of June,
That we sailed upon the waters clear,
  Beneath the rising moon.
We had often sat together thus,
  Young Lawrence Grey and I,
And watched the Night-Queen rolling
  Through her kingdom in the sky.

He spoke as he was wont to speak,
  In whispers soft and low,
Of moonlit skies and slumbering flowers,
  And wavelets' murmuring flow.
In vain I listened for the words
  I longed to hear him say;
He breathed them not,—my heart was sad,—
  I loved young Lawrence Grey.

Long had I known him; oft had sat
  Within the leafy grove,

And hoped to hear him whisper low
   An earnest tale of love;
Or stood, expectant, by his side,
   At twilight's stilly hour,
And felt across my senses steal
   A spell of wondrous power.

But Hope, the siren, from my heart
   Had well-nigh ta'en her flight;
And dark despair sat brooding there
   Upon that summer's night.
And when, at last, a sacred hush
   Fell upon wood and stream,
My thoughts were busy with the past,
   While Lawrence seemed to dream.

I touched the water with my hand,
   And tried to catch each gem
That, with the moonbeams, formed a gay,
   A sparkling diadem.
A sudden fancy seized my brain,—
   " Suspense is worse than death;
'Twill test his love to run the risk,—
   I can but lose my breath."

One parting glance was all I gave;
   But he beheld me not,

So closely were his senses bound
   By deep, unfathomed thought.
"Forgive me, Heaven!" I softly said;
   "Now love or death must win!"
And, with the words, the skiff upset,
   And I—I tumbled in.

One moment dark dismay became
   A tenant of my breast;
Another, every doubt gave way,—
   All fear was lulled to rest.
A strong arm bore me to the shore,
   Upheld my sinking form,
While tear-drops fell upon my cheeks
   All fresh and bright and warm.

"Gone, almost gone!" he wildly said,
   And smoothed my dripping hair;
Then pressed his lips upon my own,
   And left love's signet there.
A 'wildering bliss, an untold joy,
   Across my being stole;
And eyelids, that till then were closed,
   No longer brooked control.

"Lawrence!" I slowly, feebly said,—
   A flush suffused his cheek;

Then, quick, he told me all his lips
    Had long refused to speak:
He said he worshiped—he adored;
    If I would be his own,
Henceforth his aim in life should be
    My happiness alone.

What answered I? Ask of the moon,
    That now, all radiant, shone;
Or of the still, pale stars beyond,
    That tremblingly looked on.
I've tried a thousand times to think,
    But tried, alas! in vain;
Those words escaped from Memory's chart,
    And ne'er came back again.

'Twas not till many years had fled
    With many joys away,
And I had long been known to friends
    As "sober Nelly Grey,"
That I could venture to confess,
    To him who used to dream,
That it was not an accident—
    My falling in the stream.

He scarce believed me when I said
    I made the skiff capsize;

Or that I heard the words he spoke
   Before I oped my eyes.
He smiled, though, when he heard me say,
   " If I were young once more,
And loved and doubted, I would act—
   Just as I did before."

I'LL MEET THEE ALONE.

WHEN morn's rose-light lingers
   On love's hallowed bowers,
And zephyr's light fingers
   Awaken the flowers;
When echo, repeating
   Each bird's gladsome tone,
Makes joyous our hearts, love,
   I'll meet thee alone!

When Day's course is ended,
   And, from heaven's high spars,
By angels suspended
   And fastened by stars,
Hangs twilight's soft curtain,
   O'er earth's bosom thrown,
I'll hide 'neath this veil, love,
   And meet thee alone!

When Luna's soft glances
   Illumine the night,

When, as she advances,
    The stars steal from sight ;
When mortals are dreaming
    Of sweet moments flown,
I'll hasten away, love,
    And meet thee alone !

Then to our soul's vision,
    In rose-tinted dyes,
Like some fair elysian,
    The future will rise.
And—strange ears may ope, love,
    To catch my low tone ;
So, waiting, I'll hope, love,
    To meet thee alone !

LITTLE GEORGIE BALL.

FOLD the snowy cover under,
  Where his pulseless form is laid,
Then sit down to sigh and wonder
  Why this sudden call was made.
Lay the dimpled hands together
  Gently as you bend to weep,
Murmuring oft, in whispers tender,
  "Little Georgie's gone to sleep."

Why, it seems but yester-morning
  That his merry laugh rang out
As he passed, and, backward turning,
  Answered Josey's joyous shout.
Never once I dreamed, poor mother,
  Of the shadow dark and deep
Soon to fold the "little brother"
  In that icy, dreamless sleep.

Josey still keeps watching, waiting,
  Both at morn and twilight gray,

Asking, while their sports relating,
   "Why don't Georgie come to play?"
Then I fold my arms about him,
   Praying I may hold and keep;
Saying, "You must play without him, .
   Little Georgie is asleep."

Weeping mother, doting father,
   Crushed and bowed by wild despair,
Lift your eyes above the casket,
   Naught but dust is prisoned there !
Know that He who took your darling
   Will his deathless spirit keep,
Blest and happy with the angels,
   Safe till ye are called to sleep.

Then prepare to rise and meet him
   When your summons comes to go;
Wheresoe'er your treasure resteth,
   There your spirit-longings flow.
It was kind the pitying Father,
   Knowing he to wait must weep,
Took him ere earth's sorrows found him,—
   Lulled his precious form to sleep.

THE NEW YEAR.

HARK! a phantom bell is tolling, and it tolls a funeral
    chime,
While a footfall totters slowly down the corridor of Time,
To the music of a requiem from the ocean and the shore,
And from dead and shrouded forests, sighing, "Never—
    nevermore!"
Whence, oh whence this wail of sorrow,—whence this
    universal sigh,
Paling all the stars that tremble in a cold December sky?
Why, with white hair wildly streaming, comes old Time
    upon the blast,
As if marshaling his army from the ages of the Past?

See, he veils his furrowed features as he rends the gloom
    apart,
And the pall of Midnight hideth the cold form upon his
    heart;
And he groans, until his anguish fills the air with dire
    alarms,
As he treads upon the darkness with the dead Year in
    his arms.

E*

Soft! keep silent! he is pausing at the grave's eternal
    brink!

Does the yawning gulf appall him?   Does the blackness
    make him shrink?

No! his ghostly eyes are dimming, and he mourns the
    fallen one

As the king of old lamented o'er his lost and erring son:

"Thy race is run, my stricken one; thy fleeting life is
    o'er;

Thy Summer breeze and Autumn skies will come to us no
    more.

The last day of thy circling round has melted into night,

And viewless spirits wait the knell to bear thee from my
    sight.

"What hast thou seen, my cold, dead Year, since first I
    led thee forth,

And bade thee turn thy wondering gaze upon the slumber-
    ing earth?

Ah me! that bell—that phantom knell—is tolling, tolling
    slow,

As if to answer in thy stead, ' Far less of joy than woe.'

"'I've seen,' it moans, in dismal tones, 'the warring
    waves by night;

Have watched the gallant, wounded ship go down and
    out of sight;

Have seen the foaming billows rave and cleave the totter
     ing deck,
While dying creatures, ghastly pale, clung wildly to the
     wreck.

" ' I've seen the lurid lightning hurled among the frantic
     waves,
As if a torch were flung from heaven to light the ocean
     caves,
And, when the fury of the blast lashed his huge ribs apart,
I've tried to count the giant throbs that wrenched old
     Ocean's heart.

" ' I've watched the valiant soldiers fall beneath the leaden
     rain,
When no sustaining arms were near to soothe their dying
     pain ;
Have seen the homes made desolate by grim, insatiate
     War,
And wondered if 'twas justified before Jehovah's bar.'

" What hast thou heard, my stricken one, what sounds
     have met thine ear,
Since first arose my parting wail above the buried year?
Again that knell—that spirit bell—is tolling, tolling slow;
It speaks for thee still mournfully, ' Far less of joy than
     woe !'

" 'For squalid Poverty and Want have stalked throughout
  the land,
And skeletons of Pomp and Pride skulked by on every
  hand !
And from the city's crowded mart, as from the barren
  moor,
The prayer has risen, "O God of heaven, have mercy on
  the poor !"

" 'I've heard the widow's plaintive moan, the orphan's
  cry for bread,
The groans of helpless age, low-stretched on Misery's
  stony bed,
Have heard from girlhood's pallid lips the wail that slow
  decay
Wrings from the soul as, drop by drop, the life-tide ebbs
  away.'

" But, soft ! a fluttering of wings, a rustling through the
  sky,
As if the starlight trembled down to breathe a fond
  'Good-by.'
The New Year comes ! her innocence hath made stern
  purpose dumb ;
My palsied hands refuse to lift the veil of ills to come ;

For though my aged eyes have seen joy after joy depart,
To leave me naught but Memory's draught,—the wormwood of the heart,—

"Still would I screen from her young gaze the midnight
and the shade,—
The grave-yards of the human heart,—where, side by side,
are laid
Dear hopes, fond joys, aspiring dreams, that made Life's
morning bright,
But, ere its sultry noon came on, withered from early
blight.
And now farewell! I go to wait beyond the circling
years,
Where angel-harps are hung to catch the music of the
spheres;
Far up those amaranthine steeps, where flowers eternal
bloom,
I'll watch her course and gently light her pathway to the
tomb."

10

GREETING TO THE SIR KNIGHTS.

A GRAND BANQUET AND RECEPTION WAS GIVEN BY DAMAS-
CUS COMMANDERY AT KEOKUK, IOWA, OCT. 21, 1875.

WELCOME, Sir Knights! the Chapter stands
With open arms and outstretched hands!
Damascus greets, with beaming eye,
The chosen of the Mystic Tie!
And wreathes in green her banquet hall
For those who heed her kindly call.

Grand Knighthood! though not understood
The mystery of thy Brotherhood,
We know each solemn rite conferred
Is symboled in His Holy Word,
And that an origin divine
Is traced through every secret sign.

The Red Cross! not yourselves can claim
This sign alone,—'tis ours the same.
To it the sinner turns to see
The dying throes on Calvary,

And learn Redemption's price was paid
By Him on Whom our guilt was laid.

Who dares antiquity disdain
That reaches back to Bethlehem's plain?
Rolls back the ages farther still,
To rest upon Mount Zion's hill?
Claims the same paths the prophets trod,
And lifts the spirit up to God?

I AM WAITING FOR THEE.

A SONG FOR THE AGED.

BELOVÉD, dost know that, though heaven is far,
Heart throbs unto heart as star answereth to star?
That the dear ones below and the dear ones above
Receive and return mystic tokens of love?
That the mourner, though lonely, is never alone,
For a form keeps its shadow in one with his own?
Has a whisper e'er thrilled thee, a tone glad and free,
"Be patient, my own, I am waiting for thee?

"Lone heart, thou art weary! As age stealeth on
Thou longest, thou yearnest, at times, to be gone.
I read all thy thoughts, and the bright dreams I bring,
The answers to prayers 'neath my sheltering wing,
I pour on thy heart in the hush of the night,
And, hovering o'er thee, catch words of delight.
Oh, wait! and be patient till Death sets thee free,
For, darling, be *sure* I am waiting for thee.

"Yes, waiting for thee, and while thou must remain,
The summit of glory I may not attain ;
Thy love is the magnet that holdeth me near
When my spirit would soar to a loftier sphere.
Oh, not e'en for heaven would I widen the space
That holds me, at times, from the light of thy face.
I will stand at the gate, and at last thou wilt see,
When He calls thee to come, I've been waiting for thee."

10*

WOMAN'S VOICE.

WHEN sin came among us, and Eden was lone,
   The pitying Father was kind ;
For He robbed not the woman of one melting tone,
   Nor bade her leave beauty behind.
So, with all her sweet charms and her exquisite grace,
   Young Eve left that love-hallowed bower,
Retaining for Adam her beautiful face,
   And a voice full of pathos and power.

And he, although banished, though exiled for aye,
   From shades so enticing to roam,
Was not without hope, for her love was his stay,
   And her soft, witching voice was his home.
To soothe him at even with melody sweet
   Till the desert around him grew bright,
At morn his awaking with anthems to greet,
   Was her mission, her joy and delight.

Thus Woman and Melody gently combined
   To banish each lingering regret ;

Though she lured him to err and leave Eden behind,
  Resistless, he clings to her yet.
Her voice, full of sweetness, persuasive in love,
  Entrancing in cadence or swell,
Still sways him, as when, in that lost Eden grove,
  He listened and tasted and fell.

THE BROKEN-HEARTED.

ALL pale, yet beautiful in grief, she laid her down to
    rest,
And her head was softly pillowed on a loving sister's
    breast ;
A flower, exhaling to the skies, yet scarce of earth a part,
She was fading, drooping, dying,—dying of a broken
    heart.
" Tell me, sister," thus she murmured, and her whispered
    words scarce heard
Fell like strains from distant harp-strings by soft breezes
    lightly stirred,—
" Tell me, when my sands are wasted, when the silken
    cord is riven,
Will this memory cling about me? can I bear it up to
    heaven ?

" Oh, answer yes, my sister,—it were cruel to say No ;
He was false, but do not blame him, for I loved—I loved
    him so !

I have suffered keenly, deeply, but the strife is almost o'er,

And my latest thoughts now wander to the sunny days of
    yore.

Do not tell him, should he seek you, how my heart by
    grief was wrung ;

Only say, I died with blessings and his name upon my
    tongue.

Tell him how I clasped his image fondly, wildly, to my
    breast,—

How I prayed that he would join me in the mansions of
    the blest ;

How the dearest hope I cherished was, that when my soul
    was free,

Its deep love might still be changeless through a long
    eternity.

Ask him if he has forgotten the quiet, mossy dell

Where we used to sit together when the twilight shadows
    fell ;

Where he gently smoothed my tresses, drew me closer to
    his side,

Breathing low, in tenderest accents, ' Golden-haired and
    sunny-eyed.'

Where my forehead with the baptism of his lips was often
    wet ;

Ah, those moments, gone forever, how I love, how prize
    them yet !

Their remembrance lingers o'er me, the dear star-light of
    my heart,
And, though all grow dim around me, this can nevermore
    depart.

"Ask him more,—if he remembers one lovely eve in June,
How we wandered to the brook-side to watch the rising
    moon ;
How, in playfulness, his fingers traced my name upon the
    sand ;
How his own was writ beneath it in a trembling, fluttering
    hand.
Oh, he does not dream how sacredly those golden grains
    I've kept,
Or how, that moonlit evening, while others sweetly
    slept,
I glided o'er the dewy lawn, soft oped the garden-gate,
And, reaching thus the trysting-spot,—now lone and
    desolate,—
I gathered up each tiny grain, and, with a miser's care,
Concealed them with my treasured gifts,—the tress of
    auburn hair,
The picture, and the withered bud, now hidden on my
    breast,—
There, sister, let them slumber when you lay me down to
    rest.

"Softly, softly! Oh, my sister, has the daylight faded
 quite?
Or does memory now bathe me in a flood of starry light?
I can see him,—he is coming,—now his arms are open
 wide;
Lay me, sister, on his bosom! What is all the world
 beside?
Oh, I knew he would be constant! I was sure that he
 would come;
Nearer, nearer, sister—tell him—tell him—I—am—going
 —home.
You will never call him faithless—never censure, blame
 him—No!
Only tell him, sister dearest, that I loved—I *loved* him
 so!"

Her voice was hushed; 'twas over; no murmur—scarce a
 sigh;
The silence was unbroken, save by seraphs floating by.
The watcher shed no tear-drop as she closed those rayless
 eyes,
For she knew she would awaken to the joys of Paradise.
The hectic flush had faded from those snowy cheeks of
 clay,
But she thought of bloom perennial in the climes of
 endless day.

The pallid lips seemed quivering with a soft angelic smile,

As though the soul, at parting, had lingered there awhile

To breathe its benediction o'er that form of matchless
  mold,

So calm, so pure, so beautiful, so young, yet, oh! so
  cold.

And when they robed her for the tomb, they found a
  shining band

Of auburn hair,—a withered bud,—his pictured face,—
  and sand!

These, and that face so sadly sweet, a tale of suffering
  spoke;

They told how much that gentle heart was tortured ere it
  broke.

A VALENTINE.

THINK of me, darling! My poor heart seems breaking,
Saddened and crushed, by thy constant forsaking.
Never an hour but thy face is before me,
Never a day but I bend fondly o'er thee,
Never a night but my arms steal about thee,
While my heart cries, "Must I still live without thee?"
Nothing I listen to, nothing I see,
Stills, for one moment, my longings for thee.

Think of me, pet, and if thou, too, dost miss me,
Hold up thy lips, as if waiting to kiss me.
Let the good angels above us discover,
Mamma, though distant, has some one to love her.
Bid them to waft me thy kiss as a token
That the tie binding us ne'er can be broken;
E'en as the oak wooes the upreaching vine,
Yearneth my heart to be circled by thine.

F   II   121

Think of me, sweet! When the sun's golden quiver
Loosens the bands of our beautiful river,
Bend thy red lips where its wavelets are kneeling,—
Freight them with whispers of tenderest feeling,—
Let the clear waters, as thou leanest over,
Clasp thy dear image and bear me, thy lover,
Something to cheer me,—a shadow or sign,—
Something to prove thee my own Valentine.

A WELCOME TO MRS. FRANCES D. GAGE.

I WAIT thy coming, honored friend,
　With tenderness and tears,
For memory's tapers brighter burn
As age steals on, until I yearn
With confidence and trust to turn
　To friends of other years.

I've had my share of golden dreams,
　Of hopes and haunting fears;
Of days whose suns in darkness set,
Of ecstasies that thrill me yet
And make my weary heart forget
　The weight of twenty years.

The silvery threads are whiter now
　That on thy brow appear; ·
Age, suffering, and, it may be, care
Have left their spotless symbol there,
As pure as the fresh snow-flakes are
　That deck the dying year.

The shock full ripe, the golden grain
　　Awaits the Reaper's hand ;
Awaits the Boatman's silent oar—
The signal from a distant shore—
For tones of loved ones gone before,
　　Guides to the spirit-land.

The bravest heroes are not they
　　Who foremost rush to fight ;
But they who aid each glorious plan
That elevates their fellow-man ;
Who help to kindle, feed, and fan
　　The smouldering flames of Right.

More beautiful are withered hands
　　Than fingers girt with gold,
If they have scattered here and there,
With blessings oft, sometimes with prayer,
The seeds of good, henceforth to bear
　　Perchance an hundred-fold.

The tenderest and the truest hearts,
　　Strong in their purity,
Are such as crucify desire,
Forgetting self in purpose higher,

To raise humanity still nigher
  To Him who made us free.

That voice can never lose its thrill,
  Its pathos and its power,
That swells responsive to a call;
Whose earnest tones will rise and fall
In pleadings for the good of all
  Until the closing hour.

11*

OH, WHY WAS HE TAKEN?

DEDICATED TO MRS. H. SCOTT HOWELL, OF KEOKUK, IOWA.

OH, why was he taken in Life's early morning,
  Your only—your darling—your beautiful boy?
Why torn from your arms without whisper or warning,
  The babe that you counted a " well-spring of joy"?
Did you love him too much? Had the future been gilded
  With pictures too golden—with dreams all too bright?
And was it for this all the hopes you had builded
    Were shattered and crushed by Death's withering
      blight?

What is home to you now, since your hearthstone may
      never
  Be gladdened again by that innocent face,—
Since the light of his presence has vanished forever,
  And no sign of the soft, dimpled hands you may trace?
As you sit by his crib, with his playthings beside you,
  His rattle and ring and each worn, broken toy,
Your empty hearts reach for the treasure denied you,
  And your lips wait in vain for the kiss of your boy.

And you wonder, so often, if this folded blossom
In Eden's own light will unopened remain ;
When your bud is reclaimed, will you clasp to your
bosom
Your baby—the *dear, angel-baby*—again?
Will it rest on His breast, "as a child," till your coming,
In His sheltering arms Who bade children to come?
"Oh, yes!" Faith replies, as you look through the gloam-
ing :
"Not lost—only waiting with Jesus—*at Home.*"

MY MOTHER'S GLASSES.

I opened a worn trunk yesterday,
  Sitting alone in my quiet room,
And sighed as I saw them folded away,—
The garments there,—for the form that lay
  Clad in white robes in the silent tomb.

I lifted each with the tenderest care,
  And laid them out in the morning breeze ;
The caps and 'kerchiefs she used to wear,
With keepsakes, letters, and locks of hair ;
  And paused to muse when I came to these,

The glasses that aided her aged eyes,
  Grown dim from sorrows and length of years;
  She slept, at last, and earth's mists and tears
Were changed for the brightness of Paradise.

Does she watch, I wonder, with yearning gaze,
  For one she longeth to welcome there ?
When, loosed from the fetters of earth and sin,
  128

The white-robed angels glide softly in,
    Does she mark the features the ransomed wear?

If so, how long must the watcher wait
    Till she clasps the pilgrim she longs to greet?
Must my eyes grow dim, must I tarry late
Ere I catch the gleam, near the golden gate,
    Of glances with mother-love replete?

How long till my glasses are laid aside
    To gather dust in the years to come?
To be found, perchance, at some distant day,
By those I love, who will softly say,
    "No tear-dimmed eyes in her radiant Home."

F*

THE MISSISSIPPI RIVER.

THERE is not in the wide world a river as grand
As the one whose bright waves lave my own native land ;
From the dear mother-lake which it leaves with a sigh,
And murmurs, at parting, a tender good-by,
On down to the Gulf, that, with arms open wide,
Receives to her bosom the on-rushing tide,
Repeating the vow by her lover begun,
That henceforth, forever, their lives shall be one,
There are beauty and freshness and splendor untold
On its shores, on its isles, in its ripples of gold.

Past meadow and moorland, past forest and glade,
How grandly it courses in sunlight and shade !
Reflecting the blushes of morn's rosy light,
Or set with tiaras of star-gems at night ;
So mirroring heaven that if loved ones might stray
Through portals of light in the regions of day,
Or mount its bright ramparts and fondly look down,
We might catch, in these waters, the gleam of a crown,
A glad smile of joy on a glorified face,
And white arms upheld for a tender embrace.

Say, River of rivers, what is't they implore
As thy ripples press forward to kneel on thy shore?
I see them, at morn, lowly bending in prayer,—
At even their pleadings float soft on the air.
While up through the starlight comes, tender and low,   ·
The trembling refrain of their murmuring flow.
What yearnings can move thee, what longings can start,
With heaven's own image clasped close to thy heart?

I think, when thy islands of verdure are seen,
Of Eden's still waters and pastures of green,
And feel, when my feet touch thy shore's dewy sod,
A sense of His presence, a nearness to God.
A picture floats up from thy blue waves to me
Of Him who sat down by Gennesareth's sea;
And e'en when thy storm-maddened billows mount high,
They waft me the whisper,—"Fear not, it is I."

MOUNT VERNON.

A CALL—and to Woman !
  A voice from the sod
Where Washington's spirit
  Ascended to God !
A wail from the billows
  That chant round the brave,
A sigh from the willows
  That bend o'er his grave ;
A moan from the pathway
  Long worn by the tread
Of worshiping pilgrims,
  Who kneel by his bed ;
A cry from the Nation,
  That WOMAN may come
And rescue from ruin
  Our WASHINGTON'S TOMB.

A glorious purpose—
  A mission divine,
To wrest from the spoiler
  A world-worshiped shrine ;

. A call that should thrill us
  With eager desire
To claim for his children
  The dust of their sire.
Not oft has such measure
  Of glory been ours,—
Our memories to garland
  With fame's deathless flowers;
To stamp on the tablets
  Of ages to come,
Our names as the guardians
  Of WASHINGTON'S HOME.

Float gently, proud banner,
  Where greatness is laid;
Steal soft, bugle chorus,
  Through Vernon's still shade;
Go, silence the cannon
  And muffle the drum,
For, lo! to her Mecca
  Fond WOMAN has come.
No army defends her,
  No weapons she bears,
For LOVE is her watchword,
  Embalmed with her prayers.

She kneels where the laurel
　And wild myrtle bloom,
And claims as a ransom
　Her WASHINGTON'S TOMB.

No thunder-voiced ramparts
　She rears o'er his clay,
No emblems to warn us
　Of Tyranny's sway;
No fortress, defended
　By armor or gun,
To frown o'er the ashes
　Of God's chosen one;
But the wall that encircles
　Our hero's loved grave
Shall be heart to heart banded,—
　The gentle and brave.
While the pride of the Nation
　Forever shall be
The strong love of WOMAN,—
　The shield of the free.

ONE YEAR OLD.

Sitting with my babes around me,
  And the youngest on my knee,
Gazing through the open lattice
  At the sunlight warm and free;
Thinking how my spirit doteth
  On this blessed Autumn-time,
How she loves its low-voiced whispers
  Better than the Christmas chime,
Or the babbling of the brooklet
  When it bursts its icy band,
Winter's close and Spring's returning
  Loud proclaiming through the land,—
Musing thus, my eye unconscious
  Seeks the lambkin of our fold,
And Remembrance softly murmurs,
  "She is just a twelvemonth old!"

Little hands! 'neath their light pressure
  Naught but dimples now I trace;
Trusting eyes, turned fondly upward,
  Mutely woo a warm embrace.

135

Timid lips, that ne'er have ventured
  On the first sweet, trembling word,
Fluttering voice, that utters only
  Cooings like some nestling bird,
Save when raised in mocking laughter
  As she joins the children's play,
Listening to their gleeful chorus:
  "Addie's one year old to-day!"

Tottering feet, that claim the guidance
  Of a mother's guarding hand;
Tiny form, that bends and trembles
  In its weak attempts to stand;
Will that hand be spared to guide thee
  Onward through the coming years?
Will her voice be near to banish
  All thy childish doubts and fears?
Precious one! when slumber binds thee
  Thoughts like these so often start,
For there's many a secret longing
  Prisoned in a mother's heart.

Should this be, O Father! aid me
  In the truths I would impress;
When I crave Divine Assistance,
  Deign to hearken and to bless.

Sooner than these feet should wander
   Wayward, erring, from the Right,
Or these hands in acts of kindness
   Never learn to take delight ;
Sooner than these lips should utter
   Slander base or black untruth,
And this spotless soul be sullied
   In the golden hour of youth ;
Sooner, though the pang it cost me
   Might be more than I could bear,
Would I see the death-dew gather
   Now upon her forehead fair ;
Sooner, when the spring-time cometh,
   Part the grass above the mold,
Reading on the tablet o'er her :
   "Little Addie, one year old."

12*

OH, WHAT SHALL BE MY SONG
TO-NIGHT?

Oh, what shall be my song to-night?
   The earth, the sea, or sky,
The star-gems, with their trembling light,
   Or night-bird's plaintive cry?
Not such can fill the lonely heart
   With thoughts of bliss divine;
Not such a holy thrill impart
   To spirit warm as thine.

The dawning of a lovely form
   Upon the raptured eye;
The hand's soft touch, so true and warm,
   The red lip's answering sigh;
The gentle voice for which we yearn
   In crowds or lonely dell,
The beaming eye to which we turn
   Enthralled by beauty's spell,—

These be the burden of my song,
   While dreams of heaven are thine,

Made glorious by the angel throng
  Bowed at an earthly shrine.
Then turn thee once from them to-night
  To one who wanders free,
To sing how all things pure and bright
  Have found a home in thee.

LINES

WHEN the dwelling is completed
   That we haste to rear for thee,
Reverend Father, place this symbol
   Where, at morn, thou bend'st the knee;
When at eve thy low petitions
   For thy people softly rise,
Let them touch this blessed emblem
   As they journey to the skies.

May thy life be pure and holy!
   May thy faith be firm when tried!
May'st thou take for thy example
   Him they scourged and crucified!
May'st thou learn, in every trial,
   Be it danger, pain, or loss,
While the billows surge around thee,
   To cling only to His cross!

VOICELESS PRAYER.

All their childish sports were over,
  All their mimic work was done,
And they came and knelt beside me,
  Hushed and solemn, one by one.
Meekly were their soft hands folded,
  And, with young heads lowly bowed,
Softly fell their " Our Father,"
  As a star-beam through a cloud.

When the solemn prayer was ended,
  And the last " Good-night" was told,
From my lap the baby clambered,
  Tiny waif, a twelvemonth old.
Dimpled hands were clasped together,
  Blue eyes raised with reverent grace,
While a look of sweet devotion
  Gathered on his cherub face.

Wherefore came that mute appealing?
  Wherefore was his white soul stirred,

Ere his crimson lips had parted
   With the first low, trembling word?
Could an earnest wish be prisoned
   In the Eden of his heart?
Did a prayer for heavenly guidance
   From that stainless spirit start?

"Uttered not, yet comprehended,
   Is the spirit's voiceless prayer,"
To my ear the whisper floated
   As I watched him kneeling there;
Gazed and murmured, "Meet for heaven
   Are the prayers of such as he;
Innocence, in silent pleading,
   At the throne of Purity."

Then I thought of all the lessons
   Taught by Him, the Undefiled;
Most I loved His simple sermon
   With this text, "A little child."
And these sacred words seemed uttered:
   "Humble, trusting, free from sin,
As the babe who kneels beside thee,
   Must thou be to enter in."

GONE TO SLEEP.

LITTLE GEORGIE HUSSY, OF DES MOINES, IOWA, WHO DIED DURING HIS MOTHER'S ABSENCE FROM HOME.

Drop the curtain gently, softly !
  Shut the golden sunlight out ;
Bid the merry children, passing,
  Hush their laugh and joyous shout.
Lay aside the snowy cover
  Over which light shadows creep,
Then draw near and murmur over,
  " Little Georgie is asleep !"

Oh ! 'tis hard for thee, poor mother,
  Bending o'er thy darling now ;
Covering with earnest kisses
  Icy lips and marble brow,—
Hard to come and find the treasure
  Thou hadst hoped to hold and keep,
Cold and quiet in his casket,
  Bright eyes hidden—fast asleep !

Yet remember, when thou bendest
   O'er his crib and empty chair,
When the yearning love within thee
   Cries from anguish and despair,
That the One who called him upward
   Will thy precious lambkin keep ;
Only to earth's cares and sorrows
   Has thy darling gone to sleep !

GRANDMOTHER DICKEY.

It was years ago one October day
When a shadow fell on my Life's bright way;
And, with fond hopes blighted and glad dreams fled,
I turned with a weary, desolate tread
To the home I had left with light step and free,
Where my mother waited and prayed for me.

Ah! though crushed by woe, not of all bereft
Can we ever feel while this friend is left.
The love of a mother is strong and true,—
Unchanged, undiminished, our whole life through:
And her circling arms are our truest stay
When hopes we have cherished have passed away.

"Grandmother Dickey," an aged dame,
Walked over to see me the day I came:
It was life's October with grandmother then,
While mother had passed her threescore and ten.
And they both would fain have soothed me there,
As I sat beside them in mute despair.

"Grandmother" said it would not be long
Till my call would come from the ransomed throng;
Life was only a span, and 'twould be so sweet
For friends, long parted, again to meet.
And she told me my duty was plain and clear
To comfort the dear ones left me here.

Then we all knelt down, the pilgrims twain,
With me between them; and not in vain
Were the fervent prayers, as on bended knee
They asked the Father to comfort me.
For, like perfume wafted from fields of balm,
There came o'er my spirit a wondrous calm.

This was years ago, and a long, long while
It seemed as I passed o'er the grave-yard stile,
And on through the leaves of brown, crimson, and gold
That covered the graves from the Winter's cold;
Then sat me down where the maples wave
Their shadowy boughs o'er my mother's grave.

And my thoughts went back, as I bowed me there,
To an aged form, bent in earnest prayer;
And I said, She is old now as mother was then,—
If she lives, she has counted threescore and ten.

And musing thus, with my lifted eyes
Fixed on the dreary October skies,
I stood, while the branches above poured down
Their wealth of crimson and gold and brown;
Then turned to follow the sound they gave,
And to watch them fall on a new-made grave.

A rustling of feet 'mid the leaflets sere
Made me turn to look,—'twas a child drew near.
"Come hither, my lad! Whose grave? Pray tell!"
"Why, GRANDMOTHER DICKEY'S: you knew her well.
She was old and feeble and wanted to go,
For so many were dead that she used to know."

I measured the space. I was just between
The pilgrims' graves, as that day I had been
Between the twain when her voice arose
To the pitying Father to soothe my woes.
But the lips were silent that prayed for me
Whom Faith had forsaken on Life's rough sea.

And my heart wailed out a despairing moan,—
A cry for the earth-love forever flown;
Until mother's voice through the silence came,
"Waiting and praying, love, all the same."
And then "Grandmother's" words, "It will be so sweet
When friends, long parted, again shall meet!"

"THE EASTERN STAR."

READ BEFORE THE MEMBERS OF THIS DEGREE AT HAMIL-
TON, ILLINOIS, ON ST. JOHN'S DAY, JUNE 24, 1875.

MOST worthy Patron, Matron, friends,
The blue sky fondly o'er us bends;
This grand old river at our feet
Listens, as if 'twould fain repeat
To distant shore or passing breeze
A murmur of our melodies.

Oh, wisely chosen, the gentle Five,
Whose spotless virtues we should strive
To imitate, that we may be
Worthy adoptive Masonry;
Worthy to learn their sacred rite
When *heavenly* Orders greet our sight;
Worthy to catch the mystic sign
When Eastern stars *below* us shine;
Worthy to learn the pass-word given
By the sweet Sisterhood of heaven,

When golden gates are open wide,
By loved ones on the other side.

Mizpah !* the very name is fraught
With sweet significance ; for thought
Carries the heart to other years ;
The circlet on the hand appears
As first it glowed when, "Only thine,"
Responded to the mystic sign.

On Gilead's mount the maiden stood,
Not dreaming of the vow of blood
That bound her, in her budding bloom,
To meet a dread, unaltered doom.
The father came, exultant, back,
Hoping a pet-lamb on the track
Would, bounding, welcome his return ;
But, ah ! sad fate the truth to learn !
His lovely child, with flying feet,
Hastened, her honored sire to meet.

Then Jephthah told his vow, and said,
"Would that my life might serve instead !"

* "Mizpah" is often engraved in engagement-rings ; for meaning, see
Gen. xxxi. 49.

13*

But the proud daughter answered, " No !
'Twas to the Lord,—it must be so."

That answer stands, a first Degree,
In our adoptive Masonry.

O Constancy ! bright badge of love,
Ruth did thy mighty fullness prove.
" Where'er thou goest I will go ;
Thy resting-place I, too, must know ;
Thy fate, thy country, I will try,
And where thou diest I will die."
Forsaking Moab's dewy sod,
Her kindred and her people's God,
Of faithful Mahlon's love bereft,
Her fond heart had Naomi left.

" Esther, my queen ! what wilt thou, say?
If half my kingdom, I obey !"
The golden sceptre near her bent,
Admiring numbers gazed intent ;
She, kneeling, touched the shining thing,
And cried, " My people ! O my king !"
Fidelity to kindred shone
In every feature, and her tone,
Though tremulous, was firm and brave
As the fond look of love she gave.

The Crown and Sceptre thus find place
Whene'er our third Degree we trace.

"Hadst *Thou* been here, he had not died!"
Weeping, the trusting Martha cried;
"Yet, even now, O blessed Lord,
My soul hangs trembling on Thy word!"
Oh, love sublime! Oh, wondrous power,
To stay her in affliction's hour!
Her white arms, raised in mute appeal,
Her spirit's eager hope reveal.

She sees,—she feels her Saviour nigh,
And Faith repeats its yearning cry:
"I know that he will rise again,
Yet even *now*,"—and not in vain
The sweet voice plead,—she led the way
To where the lifeless Lazarus lay;
And then across His brow there swept
A mortal sorrow,—*Jesus wept.*
Then His diviner nature spoke:
"Lazarus, come forth!" The dead awoke
To learn a woman's faith could prove
The largeness of a Saviour's love,
To learn His pitying heart could melt
When those He loved in anguish knelt.

Our broken Column,—fourth Degree,
Is type of Death in Masonry;
The Evergreen, its shaft beside,
Emblem of fields beyond the tide,
Where, in Fidelity complete,
Sits Martha at her Saviour's feet.

"Forgive them, Father! they are blind!"
Thus prayed Electa, ever kind;
Her husband, children, home were gone,
Yet, brave and true, she stood alone.
The tender hands that gently led
The needy in, the hungry fed,
That prisoned in their fervent hold
The wretched wanderer, pinched and cold,
That held her hospitable Cup
To famished lips so bravely up,   •
Those hands condemned (so soft and fair)
The Crucifixion pang to bear!

Her perfect confidence in God,
Her sweet submission 'neath the rod,
Form, of her attributes, the key
To ope our sacred fifth Degree.

Lo! in the East the Magi saw
The star, and, filled with holy awe,

They followed, in their winding way,
To where the Babe of Bethlehem lay.
A woman's hand its brow caressed,—
'Twas pillowed on a woman's breast;
While its first look of pleased surprise
Found answer in a woman's eyes.

Then, may not Woman bear a part
In Masonry's exalted art?
And what bright emblem, near or far,
Significant as Eastern Star?
Our Worthy Matron long has stood
Crowned with her badge of Motherhood,
And knows full well the rapturous bliss
That woke with Mary's welcoming kiss.

Our Worthy Patron guardian stands,
Ready to guide with willing hands;
Explaining Emblem, Signet, Hue,
Exhorting us to honor true,
Telling how widowed Ruth could glean
Humbly the golden sheaves between;
Extolling Martha's changeless trust,
When life had sought its kindred dust;
Recalling Esther's pleading tone,
That moved Assyria's mighty throne;

G*

And holding, like a crystal cup,
Electa's pure devotion up.

Be' ye, my sisters, tender, true,
As our sweet type, the Violet blue ;
Steadfast as flower that ne'er will shun
The rising nor the setting sun.
Pure as the spotless Lily shine ;
Changeless and bright as leaves of Pine ;
Fervent of soul as Life can be
When warmed by glowing Charity.

Friends, brothers of the mystic tie,
Can we, unnoticed, pass you by ?
You, who have dried the widow's tears
And hushed the trembling orphan's fears ?
Who, linked as in a golden band,
With widening circles fill our land ?
Can aged eyes, though dimmed by tears,
Shut out the home that still appears
Changeless and bright to memory's view
As when both life and hope were new ?
Can the fair bride forget the tone
That answers fondly to her own ?
Or sister from remembrance tear
An elder brother's constant care ?

Till this can be will we disclaim
That Masonry is but a name ;
Till this can be we'll chant afar
The praises of the Eastern Star,
That led the wandering shepherds on
Until, at the awakening dawn,
It rested, like a royal gem,
Upon the brow of Bethlehem.

TWENTY-ONE.

AFFECTIONATELY INSCRIBED TO MY NEPHEW, S. A.

HERE is my hand, young kinsman,
  Proffered with right good will ;
And this my wish,—that coming years
  Fall round thee cloudless, still.

'Tis something to enroll the Past,
  On Memory's golden chart,
In characters whose hallowed light
  Will cheer the aged heart.

'Tis this ennobles Manhood,—
  To give the moments back
As bright and fair as when they dawn
  On Youth's bewildering track;

To let each passing record show
  A purpose strong and true,
A soul above temptation's snares,
  A tender heart and true.

I may not read thy future :
   And yet the siren Hope
Spreads out before my longing gaze
   A pleasing horoscope.

No shadow falls across thy path,
   E'en to life's setting sun,
But every promise seems fulfilled
   Thou gav'st at twenty-one.

OLD SETTLER'S SONG.

TUNE, "WAY DOWN UPON THE SWANEE RIVER."

RIGHT here, where Indian fires were lighted,
    Long, long ago ;
Where dusky forms, by rum incited,
    Danced wildly to and fro ;
We, Old Settlers, come to greet you,
    Proffer heart and hand ;
Breathe, too, a fervent prayer to meet you
    Yonder, in the spirit-land.

Gone tawny chief, whose war-cry sounded—
    All but his name,
That far and near has been resounded,
    Linked with our rising fame.
Keokuk ! with pride we gather
    On thy golden strand ;
While from the skies a loving Father
    Blesses our sunset land.

158

O brothers! there are dear old faces
    Hid 'neath the mold;
Forms missing from their wonted places,
    Hands we have clasped, still and cold.
While the scores of years behind us
    Tell we're hastening on,
And that, when friends return to find us,
    Softly may fall, " They are gone."

Here, brothers, where our noble river
    Chants through its waves,
May we remain till called to sever,—
    Make here and guard our graves.
And with welcoming shouts we'll greet you
    When you reach heaven's strand ;
Fling wide the golden gates and meet you,
    Brothers in the Eden-land.

RECOLLECTIONS OF PITTSBURG.

AROUSE thee, my muse !
From thy lethargy start,
And weave into words
What thou'lt find in my heart.
Let thy harp be new-strung,
And obey my command,
To sing me a song
Of my own native land,—
Of the clime where I roamed,
With a heart light and free
As the ripples that dance
On the breast of the sea ;
Where I flitted along
With my innocent dreams,
As free as the breezes
That dimpled our streams.

Where, stretched on the greensward,
Grown weary of play,

I slept through the noon
  Of the long summer's day.
Where winter brought sledges
  And mountains of snow ;
And bridged all the streams
  In the valley below.
Where I wished some good fairy
  Would give me the power
To turn to a zephyr,
  A bird, or a flower ;
A sunbeam—a dewdrop,
  A sprite free and wild ;
It mattered not what
  So I was not a child.

How well I remember
  How urchins, in crowds,
Would scale some tall spire
  That seemed reaching the clouds,
To prove to the timorous,
  Waiting below,
To what wonderful heights
  Silken bubbles could go !
What shouts rent the air
  When each miniature thing

14*

Rode off on the wind,
　　With the pride of a king!
What wondrous surmises
　　By all were begun,
As to where it would stop,—
　　At the moon, stars, or sun!

Then the hill that surrounded
　　The "City of Smoke;"
What scenes of enchantment
　　Its vistas awoke!
The meeting of waters,—
　　The trio in view;
Their jeweled hands clasping,—
　　How steadfast, how true,
The union of hearts,
　　Whose High-Priest was the sun!
Whose vows were, "Henceforward,
　　Name, purposes, *one!*"
What wonder that picture
　　In memory is laid,
Too faithful to perish,
　　Too constant to fade.

I've a brother (God bless him!)
　　Whose joy used to be

To sit in the twilight
   With "Sis" on his knee,
And tell her in whispers
   Of angels of light
Floating down through earth-shadows
   To watch her by night;
That no good little girl
   Need be ever afraid,
For His arms were about her
   In sunlight and shade;
That even the babe
   On a fond mother's breast
Nor shudders, nor shrinks,
   When He calls it to Rest.

Years have fled, and now "Sis"
   Has to matronhood grown;
While the "brother" calls sons
   In ripe manhood his own.
But those lessons of Faith,
   His sweet pictures of Trust,
Will live when the lips
   That portrayed them are dust.
With the wealth of the Indies
   Can never be bought
The rapturous bliss
   Of each beautiful thought,

That has sprung from the seed
 That were sown in Life's spring,
When no grief bowed my spirit
 Nor trammeled its wing.

'Tis a chilling remembrance,
 (It frightens me yet,)
The day I trudged homeward
 Distressingly wet;
Had played truant from school,
 And, most shocking of all,
Had taken a bath
 In our famous canal.
"How father will threaten!
 How mother will scold!"
I whispered, while trembling
 From terror and cold,
And when sister came in
 And wet garments descried,
"Oh, my!" I returned to her
 "Sis, you must hide."

How gently and softly
 In bed was I laid,
And never was told
 The excuse she had made!

Yet that night, when our household
  All quietly slept,
I knew that my mother
  Bent o'er me and wept.
One tender hand lifted
  My pillow of down,
The other moved soft
  O'er my tresses of brown,
While lips that might banish
  My dream, did they speak,
Left the seal of their pardon
  And love on my cheek.

I am changed from the truant
  Of life's early spring;
Am no longer a dreamer,
  A light-hearted thing.
Yet, could Fancy transport me
  To where I command,
I'd be off in a trice
  To my own native land.
Would fly to the common,
  And search for the swing;
Would clamber the hill-side,
  And drink at the spring;
On the meeting of waters
  Would gaze with delight,

And watch the balloons
  As they hurry from sight;

Would haste to the homestead,—
  The homestead—ah me!
Where now are the boughs
  Of our family tree?
No father to welcome,
  No mother to bless;
No sister to shield,
  And no brother's caress;
The hearthstone deserted,—
  The love-light all fled;
The children far distant,
  The parent tree—dead.
While the dreamer of old,
  With her lyre in her hand,
Essayeth to sing
  Of her dear, native land.

WELCOME TO TEACHERS.

SCULPTORS of the finest marble,
    Molders of our plastic youth,
Sowers of such seed as ripen
    Into everlasting truth,
Shepherds with the noblest calling
    To be found in Life's broad way,
Welcome! and may Heaven pour blessings
    On your sacred cause to-day.

Be not weary of well doing!
    Help, encourage, guard, and—*wait;*
For you hold in trust the future
    Of our young and rising State.
Whether, 'mid her regal sisters,
    She the queen or vassal be,
Ye must say, for ye are molding,
    Through our youth, her destiny.

Like our broad, unbounded prairies
   Be your efforts, large and free ;
Like our noble, chainless river,
   As it courses to the sea,
Be your words to thrill their spirits,—
   Words that rouse the daring soul ;
Words that wake to life and action
   Giant thoughts that spurn control.

Ask ye not a higher calling
   Than the work ye dare to do,
For remember your Redeemer
   Was a lowly teacher, too.
And upon these days that point us
   Far away to Bethlehem's plain,
Most of all we feel a Saviour
   Neither lived nor died in vain.

As ye thus recall the lessons
   That His daily walks reveal,
Imitate His self-denial,
   Imitate His holy zeal;
Then your years of patient labor
   Will return you golden grain ;
Ripened fields will bow in token
   That ye have not toiled in vain.

CENTENNIAL.

THE scorching August rays fell fast,
As through a Western village passed
A youth, who bore, through sun and flame,
A banner bearing high the name,
     "Centennial."

The love that lit his lifted eye
Revenge and malice might defy,
And whether met by young or old,
His answer followed, firm and bold,
     "Centennial."

"Trust not Republicans, my son,"
An agéd Copperhead begun;
"They lurk along the mountain-side."
But, jubilant, his voice replied,
     "Centennial!"

"Beware of 'Rebs,'" old Croaker cries;
"Beware of traitors in disguise!"

But opening wide his arms for all,
He shouts aloud the magic call,
                    "Centennial!"

And later, when, his goal attained,
He paused where sunset's glory waned,
His whisper floated to the stars
That hid behind those crimson bars,
                    "Centennial."

The young moon, too, too coy to speak,
Dropped golden kisses on his cheek;
Then, as he slept, she veiled her light
And murmured, with her soft "Good-night,"
                    "Centennial."

And thus, by Heaven's own touch caressed,
In dreams our hero's footfalls pressed
The golden streets, where patriots heard,
And softly breathed our Union-word,
                    "Centennial."

EIGHTEEN HUNDRED AND SIXTY-TWO.

I'D a dream last night: in the dim twilight
 I was thrilled by a strange emotion;
For the Old Year came, with his withered frame,
And led me on by a torch of flame
 To the verge of the pathless ocean.

In our onward flight, by the lurid light
 Beamed his eye with a spectral brightness;
And he shivered so in the drifting snow,
While his silvered hairs fluttered to and fro
 O'er a forehead of ghostly whiteness.

Yet he made no moan as we hurried on,
 While the stars bent, pitying, o'er him;
Though from rock and dell rose a parting knell,
And the weird trees whispered a low farewell
 As their shadows knelt before him.

But he paused with me by the grand old Sea,
 Where the Night in her glory slumbered;

And he gathered sand from the golden strand,
And said, as it dropped from his palsied hand,
   "'Tis thus that my hours are numbered.

" Yet before I go to my couch of snow
   I will sing, though my voice may quiver ;
For my heart is brave as you dauntless wave
That laughs ere it leaps to its ocean grave,
   To be locked in its depths forever.

" But no thought of earth, with her joy and mirth,
   Upon memory's page is beaming ;
Not her sweet spring flowers, or her summer hours,
Or the whispered echoes from love-lit bowers,
   Or her bright autumnal gleaming.

" For these strains are old, you have heard them told
   By the years that have dawned and perished ;
And the witching ways of their smiling Mays,
And their golden, dreamy October days,
   Are like those I once fondly cherished.

" So my voice shall sweep to the boundless deep,
   Far down 'neath the wild waves hoary,

That madly tore from their glittering floor
The magic chain, lest the listening shore
  Might learn of their viewless glory.

*   *   *   *   *   *   *

" Then list to me, and I'll sing to thee
Of the mystic depths where I've wandered free ;
Of the coral halls and the diamond bed
Where old Neptune sits with his pale-faced dead ;
Of the fairy grottoes of gold and pearl,
That the sea-nymphs weave for each fair young girl
That the storm-king bears from the ocean's crest
And lays, in her beauty, down to rest.

" Oh, wonderful things have I seen below,
Where the bright fern clings and the sea-flowers blow ;
Where the mermaids gather and slyly hide
Their red-lipped shells from the amorous tide ;
Where shattered wrecks, with their gold-heaped spars,
On the pebbles gleam like a heaven of stars.

" There is one bright spot that I love to scan :
'Tis the emerald couch of a valiant man,
Whom the breakers' roar nor the flame-lit sky,
Nor the prayers of kindred, could urge to fly.

'The ship's on fire!' like a funeral knell
On the hearts of that startled crew it fell;
And strong men shook, as the lurid glare
On the waters gleamed like a hideous stare;
And women shrieked, as with fiendish sound
The fiery serpents hemmed them round,
And hissed in glee as their fangs were pressed
Through the babes that slept on their mothers' breast.
But the brave commander, with dauntless mien,
At the helm of the sinking ship was seen;
And when maddened flames through the crackling shrouds
And the hot air leaped till they licked the clouds,
When the whirlwind force of the tempest's breath
Swept the tottering wreck in the jaws of death,
With the firm, strong grasp of an iron will
He clung to the mast, and he clings there still.

"The beautiful maidens adown the main
Have tried to untwine his grasp in vain;
They made him a couch of the greenest moss
And the snow-white down of the albatross;
And they placed at the head, for a funeral stone,
The shell that could utter the softest moan;
And they tried to melt in their gentle hold
The icy touch of those fingers cold.
But they found it vain; so with tender care
They wove a pillow of sea-weeds there,

And, circling around it, these matchless girls
Knelt as they severed their own bright curls,
And tossed them down till their sheen was pressed
By the brave man's feet they had wooed to rest.
And 'tis thus he stands, like a warrior bold,
Chained to the wreck with his iron hold.

"And far away, where the billows moan
In a sadder strain and with softer tone,
I have seen, in its infant beauty, lay
A bright creation of human clay,
As pure its cheek and its brow as fair
As dews from heaven or the snow-flakes are ;
And the dimpled hands round that cherub face
Were fondly clasped in a long embrace,
While the sleep that closed its unconscious eye
Grew deep 'neath the waves' soft lullaby.
A lonesome thing seemed that babe to me,
Rocked in the arms of the great, broad sea ;
A wee, small thing to have come so far
All by itself, without spot or scar ;
A frail, weak thing, with no hand to guide
Such tender feet down the rugged tide.
Yet I know when they launched that unguided barge
The void in its mother's heart seemed large

As the ocean's self, and her grief as wild
As the breakers dashing above her child.

" But my strain must cease :—through the starlight clear
I have heard the steps of the coming Year ;
My pulses flutter, my eye grows dim,
Yet once I was merry and strong like him.
Oh, my brighter days !—they are crowding back :
I am gazing now on Spring's rosy track,
Till the Summer comes with her broad, bright smile,
And the Autumn follows her steps the while.
But they vanish now,—yes, they all have flown,
And left me here, with the Night, alone.
I'm a frail old man,—all my bright dreams sped,
My fond hopes crushed, and my loved ones dead.
Well, my snow-couch waits me,—yon phantom bell
Is tolling slowly my parting knell.
I will rest me here where the wild waves sweep :—
Good-night, fair Earth, I—must—sink—to—sleep."

So the Old Year slept, and the New Year leaped
   From the clouds to the moaning billow ;
And he bade it stand on the golden strand,
And guide his steps with its jeweled hand
      To the agéd champion's pillow.

And the New Year bowed, while the starry crowd
    That had thronged the verge of even
Marked his earnest gaze, and in hymns of praise
They told the birth of this Prince of Days
    To the countless hosts of heaven.

And the clouds drew up, from their magic cup,
    The tears that each gentle flower
Had wept unseen when the earth was green,
And faithless zephyrs, with flattering mien,
    Went wooing from bower to bower.

And this treasured dew, when the year was new,
    They poured from their crystal chalice,
Till it touched his brow, though I scarce knew how,
Nor yet who had breathed the baptismal vow
    That rang through his midnight palace.

Then I saw him fly through the sapphire sky,
    Earth's spells and her fetters scorning,
Till he sat alone where his sire had flown,
A crownéd king on his royal throne:—
    And when I awoke—it was morning.

11*

ANGEL WHISPERS.

DEDICATED TO MY SISTER, MRS. SARAH A. AYRES.

ONE beautiful evening in summer,
   Ere the sunbeams had vanished from sight,
When they stooped down to kiss the green prairies,
   And bid all the flowers "Good-night";

When the last lingering rays that descended
   Fell full in the waterfall's face,
And caught the bright ripples, while dancing,
   To give them a parting embrace;

Sad and doubting I sat by the brook-side,
   And gazed on expiring Day,
Until Thought fell asleep in my bosom
   And Memory flew softly away.

The clouds that hung lightly above me
   Wore colors of beauty untold:
Displaying, in exquisite blending,
   Their crimson and purple and gold.

178

The Breeze had forgotten its murmur,
  The Zephyr had banished its sigh,
And echoes of heavenly anthems
  Seemed dropping from harps in the sky.

Anon came the dim, dreamy twilight
  To bend o'er our wild-flower track;
For, like truants, the sunbeams strayed earthward,
  While darkness kept drawing them back.

Soon the long, waving grass of the meadow,
  The waterfall sparkling and bright,
The trees and the church on the hill-side,
  Were hid by the curtain of Night.

Then I sighed, in the fullness of sadness,
  To think that the sunbeams had died,
Until white pinions fluttered around me,
  And low whispers woke at my side:

"The gloom that the Night casts o'er nature
  The splendor of Day ever mars,
But 'tis only the darkness, O mortal!
  Can bring out the light of the stars.

" The soul, like the heavens above thee,
　　Has its seasons of sunlight and gloom ;
And often the mental horizon
　　Is clouded by thoughts of the tomb.

" When the beams of Prosperity gladden,
　　　Our troubles are laid in the dust ;
And 'tis only Adversity's mantle
　　Can bring out the starlight of Trust.

"Go ! learn of this emblem a lesson,—
　　Let Faith find a home in thy breast,
And Contentment will follow her footsteps,
　　And sing all repinings to rest."

There was silence,—I gazed all around me
　　For the source of those whispers of love ;
But naught met my wandering vision
　　Save the stars looking down from above.

Since then, when earth-shadows enfold me,
　　New strength to my spirit is given ;
For I know it is *only the darkness*
　　Can bring out the starlight of heaven.

MY FATHER'S BIRTHDAY.

Iт is dreamy, soft October,
  And there's brightness everywhere ;
From the golden sheaves of sunlight
  Gleaming in broad fields of air,
To the sparkling, dancing ripples
  That go singing to the shore,
Breathing low, to drooping branches,
  "Sweet October's come once more."

Hallowed month ! thy lights and shadows
  Waft me back to other years ;
Thou hast led me to the greensward
  Where my childhood's home appears.
And I pause, expectant, listening
  For a footfall as of yore ;
For the tender words of welcome
  I shall hear on earth no more.

16   181

Oh, *he* loved thee, rare October,
   With thy mellow, dreamy skies!
And he called thy breezy murmurs
   Nature's soothing lullabies
To the shivering, palsied blossoms
   That she gathered to her breast,
Spreading o'er them leaves of scarlet,
   That the weary things might rest.

Ne'er till now, sweet Psalm of Autumn,
   Heard I thy familiar strain,
But I heard his voice, in chorus,
   Chant a jubilant refrain.
Mine the loss,—the mist that gathers
   Veils thy smiles but from my eyes,
For I know that he is keeping
   This October in the skies.

Has his chainless spirit wandered
   From the realms of perfect day,
Through earth's shades and damps to greet me
   Upon this, his natal day?
Oh, it is not far for loved ones
   When the silken cord is riven,
For they only close their eyelids
   To re-open them in heaven.

" Lift me up into the twilight ;"
  When my failing sight grows dim,
May the light of Faith be near me,
  As heaven's twilight was to him !
When I've quaffed the latest portion
  Of this life's mysterious cup,
May his soul be near, in waiting,
  To enfold and lift me up !

THE END OF THE RAINBOW.

WRITTEN FOR LITTLE ETTA AYRES.

"Come, Nellie!" I cried, on a clear April day,
When the sunbeams kept kissing the shadows away,
"The rainbow has lit on the hill, and, you know,
We might find heaps of gold at the end of the bow."

We were young, foolish children, sweet Nellie and I,
And we thought that the hill-top was close to the sky;
Believed, too, because we were told it was so,
We should find "lots" of gold at the end of the bow.

So onward we trudged, over meadows of green,
Whose clover-blooms brightened their emerald sheen;
Then down from the hill to the valley below,
And gazed all around for the end of the bow.

"Not here!" I said, sadly; but Nellie replied,
"It is hid in yon grass by the waterfall's side;
Run fast! if you move o'er the pebbles so slow,
I'm sure I'll be first at the end of the bow."

184

We found not the treasures we searched for till night,
But Nellie, the sweet, fragile blossom, was right;
From this valley of shades she was first called to go
To the clime where is resting the end of the bow.

Where rainbows of glory eternally play,
Our Nellie is singing with seraphs to-day;
And her beautiful pinions are folded, I know,
In the fullness of joy at the end of the bow.

16*

THE DYING SOLDIER.

WITH forehead throbbing from pain,
　　With lips that were burning and dry,
A soldier lay, between heaps of slain,
　　By his comrades left to die.
Moans! moans! moans!
　　The air reeled, sick as they fell,
Yet still he sang the " Song of the War,"
　　In the tone of a funeral knell.

" Fight ! fight ! fight !
　　Through the summer's fervid heat ;
And fight ! fight ! fight !
　　'Mid rain and snow and sleet.
Scarcely an hour to rest,
　　Scarcely an hour to pray,
　Until, like me, a comrade falls
　　In the midst of the deadly fray.

" March ! march ! march !
　　Till the limbs are numb and sore ;

And march! march! march!
  Till the feet are bathed in gore.
Grown so athirst for blood
  That, while halting, by woods or streams,
We fall asleep to meet our foes,
  And shoot them down in our dreams.

"On! on! on!
  Brave comrades, with purpose true!
Your steadfast souls must never swerve
  From the work ye dare to do.
For the Union ye must defend,—
  Ay! barter your lives to save,—
Now stands, like a reeling, tottering ship,
  On the brink of a yawning grave.

"Peace! peace! peace!
  O God! will it never come?
I can almost hear that pleading cry
  From lips now pale and dumb;
Can almost catch the words,
  As they echo, near and far,
Through the widow's plaint and the orphan's wail,
  'We have had enough of War!'

" Home ! home ! home !
   What memories o'er me steal !
It were sweet to die with the loved ones there,
   In the room where we used to kneel
And offer our evening prayer
   For those who had gone to fight ; ·
Ah me ! what a bitter time was that
   When I breathed a sad ' Good-night !'

" I think that I tasted all
   The wormwood in sorrow's cup,
When Mary covered her streaming eyes
   And held the baby up,—
When mother, so old and frail,
   Came in for a parting kiss,
And prayed we might meet in a better world,
   If not again in this.

" Home ! home ! home !
   Oh, would they were with me here !
To press their lips to my burning cheeks,
   Or dew them with a tear.
Fond heart ! it is hard to go
   When life seems so full of joy !
Who will shield my wife and the agéd one,
   And my helpless baby boy?"

With forehead throbbing from pain,
  With lips that were fevered and dry,
A soldier lay, between heaps of slain,
  By his comrades left to die.
The struggle—the fight was o'er;
  His soul, on that summer's even,
Had floated off from the field of blood,
  To Home and Peace and Heaven.

CALL ME THINE OWN.

Call me thine own, dearest,
   Call me thine own;
Whisper it over
   In love's gentlest tone.
Murmur it oft
   In the stillness of night;
Tenderly breathe it
   At morn's early light.
Naught in the wide world
   Can thrill like thy tone;
Then call me thine own, dearest,
   Call me thine own.

Call me thine own, love;
   Far dearer to me
Are such words than bright gems
   From the depths of the sea.
Like music the sweetest,
   Oft wakened before,
My heart drinks them in,
   And keeps thirsting for more.

Oh, the purest of joy
   This fond heart e'er has known,
Has been born of this thought,—
   Thou hast called me thine own.

Then call me thine own, dear;
   Embalmed with thy breath,
Those accents will linger
   To cheer me till death.
Whether severed by fate
   From the dearest and best,
Or, in rapture untold,
   I recline on thy breast,
Still, still round my path
   Let this blessing be thrown,—
That thou hast, dost, and ever wilt,
   Call me thine own.

GOD'S CANDLE.

DEDICATED TO MRS. ALICE BALDWIN, OF BURLINGTON,
IOWA, THE "LITTLE GIRL" OF YORE.

"OH, isn't it pretty?" a little girl cried,
With her bright eyes upturned, as she stood by my side.
"It is just like the moon that we both used to see
When Addie and I sat on grandfather's knee.
I wonder," she said, as I gave her a kiss,
"If God looked at that when He went to make this."

I brushed from her forehead a tiny, stray curl,
And pressed to my bosom the dear little girl;
Then told her the moon was the same she had seen
Ere she crossed the great rivers and prairies of green.
"Then why," she said, quickly, appearing to doubt,
"Does it sometimes shine brightly and sometimes go
        out?"

She paused, mused a moment, then, turning to me,
And clapping her hands in her innocent glee,

"I know *now*," she answered, in tones of delight :
" *God's candle !* He carries it with Him at night ;
He takes it through heaven wherever He goes,
And that's why it moves through the sky, I suppose.

"And I think I can guess why He brought it to-night,
And why He is looking at me by its light :
At grandfather's knee every evening I pray,
And He thinks I'll forget it because I'm away."

Then, kneeling, she murmured the prayer she was taught,
And added, "Dear Father, I have not forgot,
But please take Thy lamp while I'm praying to Thee,
And hold it for Addie, that she, too, may see."
I turned to the sky as the prayer upward flew :
A cloud hid the face of the Night Queen from view.
The little one rose, as she said, with a smile,
"I knew He would hold it for Addie awhile."

I   17

AWAY!

Away, away! thou kneel'st in vain,
  I will not hear thy plea;
'Tis worse than useless, fawning one,
  To bend the knee to me!
Too late, too late those earnest vows
  Are offered at love's shrine;
Though flowing from thy heart, they wake
  No answering tone in mine.

Away, away! I loved thee once
  With all a woman's soul;
Thou read'st it in the varying blush
  That would not brook control.
And thou didst smile a strange, cold smile
  Whene'er our glances met
That almost crushed my young life out,—
  Think'st thou I can forget?

Away, away! I spurn thee now,
  For time has burst the spell;

Thou knowest that I loved thee once,
   "Not wisely, but too well."
Hadst thou not deemed me all too weak
   To clasp to thy proud breast,
Freely would I have given all
   Affection's mines possessed.

Away, away! thou need'st not speak
   To the once "thoughtless girl;"
Thy words, if uttered, would but fall
   As rain-drops upon pearl.
Reason has triumphed, and 'twould seem
   But mockery to begin
To woo and flatter when remains
   The shade of what has been.

Away, away! another's glance
   Has fondly met my own;
Another's voice has thrilled my frame
   With its low, witching tone;
Another's lips have trembled with
   The hopes they dared confess;
Another for my hand has sued,
   And I have answered "Yes."

PARTING SONG.

SUNG BY THE GRADUATING CLASS OF THE KEOKUK HIGH
SCHOOL, MAY 3, 1872.

OUR farewell must to-day be spoken,
   The time draws near when we must part,
Yet Friendship holds our chain unbroken,
   And clasps the links that bind each heart.
And ever, in the years before us,
   Will Memory guard with jealous care
The golden hours that floated o'er us
   When youth flew by with visions fair.

While o'er the Past our thoughts are yearning,
   Our deepest gratitude is due
To him who, all our needs discerning,
   Has kept life's highest aims in view.
The guiding hand so ready ever
   To point our feet to Wisdom's way,
The voice that strengthened each endeavor,
   We leave with fond regret to-day.

196

And ere we go take our places
  'Mid changing scenes on earth's broad mart,
Love stamps these dear familiar faces
  In deathless lines on every heart.
Though future joys be crushed by sorrow,
  Though hopes be changed to doubts and fears,
Undimmed throughout our life's To-morrow
  Will gleam the light of other years.

17*

THE WORLD WANTS WOMEN.

THE world wants women, brave, reliant, true,
    Such as will help the common good along,—
Workers, to keep life's highest aims in view,
    Uphold the Right and strive to crush the Wrong.
Women to lift their erring sisters up,
    When, by the wayside, they may chance to fall ;
Women with outstretched hands to snatch the cup
    From manhood's lips, and weaken thus his thrall.

The world wants mothers, earnest hearts that feel
    True sympathy for childhood's hopes and fears ;
Lives that their wealth of tenderness reveal
    Through all the changes of the circling years.
Whether, with steadfast feet, the children climb
    Life's rugged paths, or falter on the track,
They need the magnet, wondrous and sublime,
    Of mother-love to hold or draw them back.

The world wants daughters; when the tottering feet,
    The palsied limbs, declare strength, vigor flown,

When agéd eyes are dimming, it is sweet
   To know the pilgrims journey not alone,—
That willing hands are near to gently guide';
   That loving hearts will cheer them to the vale ;
That tender voices, as they near the tide,
   Will whisper of the Love that cannot fail.

The world wants sisters, gentle, faithful, pure,
   Stronger in purpose than the hosts of sin ;
Sisters to warn, encourage, and allure
   Those who might else be led to "enter in."
Oh, turn ye, mothers, sisters, daughters, turn
   From Fashion's giddy vortex ere too late,
Strive the true aim of Womanhood to learn,
   And cease to charge your blighted hopes to *Fate*.

MAYMIE.

WHO that has seen some household idol fade
  Like opening bud before the chilling blast,
Can faintly know His sufferings when He said,
  "If Thou wilt, Father, let this cup be passed."
And whosoever, when that life hath fled,
  Can bow submissively and drain the cup,
And cry, "Thy will be done," though Hope has fled,
  Has faith enough through life to bear her up.

I knelt beside her and, despairing, prayed ;
  Her little, pleading voice caught up the strain :
"Oh, spare me, Father, for her sake," she said ;
  "Give me back life and strength and love again !"
"Or if, my Father, it seems best to Thee
  From future woe to take my treasured one,
Do as Thou wilt, for Thou alone canst see :
  Give me but faith to cry, 'Thy will be done !'"

200

I rose and kissed her while she faintly smiled;
   Her breath grew shorter and her pulse beat low;
"The morning dawneth; 'tis thy birthday, child!
   God gave thee to me just ten years ago.
Thy father laid thee in these waiting arms
   Amid the shadows of the morning dim,
And now, with all thy childhood's added charms,
   I yield, and give thee back to God and him."

The dying grasp was tightened round my own,
   As if to bear me with her in her flight;
"Thou'rt going, love," I said, "but not alone:
   He bears thee upward to the world of light.
Thy mother's voice shall be the last on earth
   To soothe her darling ere the cord is riven,
And, at thy spirit's new and glorious birth,
   Thy father's first to welcome thee to heaven."

Thus she went from us in the morning gray,
   Her earthly and her heavenly birthday one;
Leaving behind her only pulseless clay,
   And a crushed heart to cry, "Thy will be done."
We robed her, as she said, in spotless white,
   And lifted grandma for a parting kiss;
Then bore the lovely burden from her sight
   And bade the children come. How they would miss
    I*

The kindling eye, the earnest, welcoming voice,
　　The hand's warm pressure, and the beaming smile!
But they all gathered there, both girls and boys,
　　And as they stood around, and gazed, the while,
I bade them sing the songs she loved so well:
　　Their Sabbath greetings and their closing lays;
And, as their trembling accents rose and fell,
　　I felt an angel voice had joined their praise.

'Twas her delight in concert thus to meet
　　The children in the Sabbath morning's glow;
To sit and learn with them the story sweet
　　How Jesus came to bless them here below.
And can it be that never, never more,
　　Her joyful voice will join the sacred songs?
That not till I have reached the shining shore
　　My ear will catch the tone for which it longs?

Yet hush! sad heart! my loss is her release!
　　What is the school below to that above?
How will our Sabbaths here compare in peace
　　With that serener day that dawns above?
What melody, what cadence half so sweet
　　As swells when angel-fingers sweep the strings?
What prayers, with such adoring love replete,
　　As when the seraphs bow with folded wings?

While here, she loved each prophet's life to trace,
   And tell of all the trials they had passed ;
But there, she sits with Moses, face to face,
   In the fair Canaan that was his at last.
And father Abraham will not pass her by :
   I thought of Isaac all the night she died,
And asked, as searchingly I turned my eye,
   If aught for my pet lamb might be supplied.

O holy Samuel, guide her o'er the strands,
   And through the Heavenly Temple, large and fair,
Because the picture of thy claspéd hands
   In early childhood bowed her soul in prayer.
Show her where Daniel sits,—where David sings,
   In loftier measure, more seraphic Psalms,
Then lead her gently to the King of kings,
   Who bade His children here to " Feed His lambs."

And, mother Mary, I must plead with thee
   Sometimes to clasp her to thy loving breast ;
Else her fond, yearning heart will long for me,
   Though heaven be gained and all its joys possessed.
Not to the Virgin Mary do I kneel ;
   Not to the holy saint my numbers flow ;
But to the MOTHER, whose true heart can feel,
   Because it once endured a kindred woe.

And, Maymie, when thy golden harp is tried,
   When strains of love fall sweetly from thy tongue,
Fold thy white wings, and at thy Saviour's side
   Let the wild yearnings of thy heart be sung.
Kneel, darling, kneel, and ask for what thou wilt;
   I know the wish e'en angels may not smother:
Not to be made more free from sin and guilt,
   But that thy mission be to guard thy mother.

And if my spirit falter ere this cup
   Of bitterness be drained—this large supply,
Reach down thy little hands and hold me up,
   Else I must wholly sink, and, helpless, die.
Yes, darling, pray! thy earnest voice can plead
   That on thy viewless pinions thou may'st come,
To hover near, in this my greatest need,
   And then be near, at last, to guide me home.

Oh! man may climb the topmost round of fame,
   And smile in triumph on the rocky steep;
In characters of blood may write his name,
   While woman's portion is to watch and weep.
Yet who would barter all the love that glows
   With quenchless fervor in a mother's heart,
E'en though that love be bought with anguish-throes,
   For all that man can reach or wealth impart?

And even though, like mine, her hopes be crushed,
    Her blossom blighted and her day-star fled,
Though the glad voice is here forever hushed,
    And the sweet lips that sang all cold and dead,—
'Tis not in hopeless grief her head is bowed,
    'Tis not in wild despair she meets His will;
For, mounting past the coffin and the shroud,
    Her soul is mother of an angel still.

How saintly was the look her features wore
    Before I saw the coffin-lid go down!
That marble brow, I kissed it o'er and o'er,
    And left my tears among her tresses brown.
That cold, cold cheek!   Those lips, so pale and still,
    Would never more unto mine own be pressed;
Those little hands, so quick to do my will,
    Were crossed and quiet on a silent breast.

Oh! be ye guarded what ye do or say
    . Before a mother when her child is dead;
Move with hushed tread beside the pulseless clay,
    And in low whispers let your words be said.
Remember of her life it was a part;
    Remember it was nourished at her breast;
That she would guard it still from sudden start,
    The ringing footfall, or untimely jest.

We bore her back to the old home she left
   With strange reluctance only months before ;
How doubly there my poor heart seemed bereft
   To miss her smiling welcome at the door !
The constant feet that used to stand and wait
   To welcome me were gone : I could not see
Her form come bounding through the wicket-gate,
   Or hear her tones of joyful, childish glee.

We moved the sod from off her father's breast,
   And laid her down to her serene repose ;
Upon his bosom she will sweetly rest,
   As withered bud beside the parent rose.
Together may their dust be mingled there,
   E'en as their souls are knit beyond the tide !
Together may their deathless spirits share
   The boundless glory of the Other Side !

'TIS NOT DEATH.

'Tis not death, but only gliding
　Upward through the pearly gate,
Just to see that all is ready ;
　Just a little while to wait.
Just to fan the Eden bowers
　With her new-tried angel wings,
And to sweep her snowy fingers
　O'er her harp of golden strings.

'Tis not death, but only mingling
　With those bright, angelic throngs,
That the blessed ones may teach her
　All their grand, triumphant songs.
She will learn them of the angels ;
　She will know them when we come,
And, before we reach the portal,
　We shall hear her " Welcome home !"

'Tis not death, but only hastening
　To the loved ones gone before,

Just to learn how love unmeasured
  Shall be hers for evermore.
Just to feel her spirit folded
  In a father's warm embrace,
And to gaze, with joy and rapture,
  On an angel sister's face.

'Tis not death: the soul's releasing—
  Bursting of its prison bars—
Bounding back to God who gave it—
  Mounting upward to the stars—
Is but life—'tis life eternal
  Here to close the weary eyes
But to open them, with transport,
  On the beams of Paradise.

'Tis not death: we have not lost her:
  She has only gone before,
Just to hold a welcome ready
  When we reach the shining shore.
Earthly ties are loosening round us,
  Earthly hopes are laid aside;
Here in flesh, but there in spirit,—
  Heaven is home since Maymie died.

THE SADDEST THING.

I'VE done the saddest thing to-day
    That ever fell to woman's lot:
I've folded all her clothes away,
    And every treasured plaything brought
To lay beside them, one by one;
    Her birthday gifts and Christmas toys,
And then to weep, when all was done,
    O'er buried hopes and vanished joys.

Her little dress, in childish haste,
    Her own dear hands had laid aside;
Upon the pins that held the waist
    I pressed my lips, and softly cried.
Within her gaiters, 'neath my chair,
    Two half-worn, crimson stockings lay,
And with a pang of wild despair
    I bent and hid them all away.

The purple ribbon that she wore,
    The coral rings and pin were there,

And just beneath them, on the floor,
　The silken band that tied her hair.
A handkerchief that bore her name
　Was folded like a tiny shawl ;
And, wrapped within this snowy frame,
　Just as she left it, lay her doll.

It bled afresh, this wounded heart,
　As if with some new sorrow stung,
As, with a wild and sudden start,
　I came to where her cloak was hung.
I caught it, sobbing, to my breast,
　As if it held the missing form,
And in low murmurs fondly blest
　What once had kept my darling warm.

Her gentle fingers seemed to glide
　Across my brow to soothe my pain,
As from the pockets at the side
　I drew the gloves that still retain
The impress of those loving hands,
　Whose magic touch seemed fraught with power
To cheer me 'mid the scorching sands
　Of sorrow, in life's desert hour.

Her little hat no more will take
　To its embrace her sunny hair ;

I felt that my poor heart must break
　To see it lying, empty, there.
The beaming eyes it used to shade
　No more with trustful glance will shine ;
The grass the early spring hath made
　Is growing 'twixt her brow and mine.

Her silk and thimble both were laid
　With thread and scissors on the stand ;
Her dolly's dress, but partly made,
　Seemed waiting for the molding hand.
The drawing of a blighted vine,
　Torn, ruthless, from a withered tree,
Meet emblems of her life and mine,
　Were the last lines she traced for me.

Oh ! was there ever grief like this ?
　Can sorrow take a form more wild
Than sweeps across us when we miss
　The presence of a darling child ?
And is there any thought that cheers
　Like this, the heart by anguish riven,—
That Time was given to mark our tears,
　Eternity to measure Heaven ?

I MUST LEARN TO LIVE WITHOUT THEE.

I MUST learn to live without thee, must, unmurmuring,
    learn to wait
With my soul bowed down within me, weary, lone and
    desolate ;
Though my poor, crushed heart still yearneth, all her
    pleading cries are vain,
For the shining ones who took thee may not bear thee
    back again.
Oh! it seemeth so mysterious that the Father thought it
    best
Thus to rob me of my treasure, when the mansions of
    the blest
Were all full to overflowing, while around the mercy-seat
Such a multitude of voices joined in praises low and
    sweet.

I must learn to live without thee, but 'tis only for a time,—
I shall see thee, know thee, love thee, in that fairer, purer
    clime !

I will search among the angels till I find thy radiant brow,
And will fold thee to my bosom as I long to clasp thee
 now.
Thou wilt pause to bid me welcome, though the bright,
 angelic throng
May have taught thee every anthem, every full and
 glorious song,—
Thou wilt hush thy harp to greet me; thou wilt show
 me, by thy choice,
E'en the minstrelsy of heaven may not drown a mother's
 voice.

I must learn to live without thee; thou wilt watch and
 wait for me
Till the boatman comes to bear me over Death's dark,
 mystic sea;
'Twill be easier far to heed him, when his summons bids
 me come,
Than if thou wert left to mourn me in a clouded earthly
 home!
Oh! the thought of thy fond welcome is the day-star of
 my soul,
And in dreams I leap to meet thee, spurning distance and
 control;
So I am not quite forsaken, though of life and love bereft,
While thy spirit hovers o'er me and this blessed hope is
 left.

ANNIVERSARY.

When first thou went'st my yearning heart,
  With many a low, despairing cry,
Kept reaching up, with sudden start,
  As if to draw thee from the sky.
And when they said, "Be reconciled,
  And know it is the Father's will,"
I only moaned, "My child! my child!"
  And held my arms to clasp thee still.
But vain were all my pleading cries;
  My prayers, my longings, all were vain:
My wild lament might reach the skies,
  But could not call thee back again.

And time wore on; the summer days
  Dragged, with slow step, their weary length,
While upward still my earnest gaze
  Would wander as I prayed for strength.

214

I mind me when the great eclipse
   Spread its black wings o'er earth and sea,
With eager eye and parted lips
   I stood to catch a glimpse of thee.
I said, "If from the jasper wall
   The angels lean toward friends below,
Thy searching glance may on me fall,
   Thy gentle whispers soothe my woe."
But through the shade no gleam was given,
   I could but watch and yearn in vain ;
It only met the frown of Heaven,
   My wish to call thee back again.

And so, as each returning year
   Brought round the day that claimed my child,
With bursting sigh and blinding tear
   It found me still unreconciled.
It seemed so long to watch and wait :
   My selfish sorrow made me blind ;
I charged my bitter loss to *fate*,
   Nor felt the chastening Hand was kind.
The wild, wild wish to have thee here,
   Close to my heart, in joy or pain,
Was all I craved,—to feel thee near,
   To have thee, darling, back again.

But now, oh now, I see it all
　　With vision clear, with open eyes,
And would not, if I could, recall
　　Thy deathless spirit from the skies.
Nor will I think the blight and gloom
　　That sear and shade a world like ours,
Are known to those who rest in bloom
　　And brightness in the Eden bowers.
Forever safe, forever blest,
　　'Tis sweet to know thou wilt remain ;
And from that true, abiding Rest
　　I would not call thee back again.

LINES ON RECEIVING MAYMIE'S PICTURE.

ARTIST, I thank thee for the pictured face,
Thy genius untranscended bade thee trace;
The perfect image of the darling one
Who waits for me when life's sad dream is done.
How bitter my regret, when last I pressed
Her marble cheek unto my yearning breast,
To feel that never more those earnest eyes
Could give returning look of glad surprise;
That never more those pale, cold lips could press
Mine own in their outgushing tenderness!
And when they thought to comfort me, and said
That was but dust,—the soul forever fled,—
It made me yearn more wildly for the clay,—
The precious features they had hid away.
One sunny tress was all that I might claim
To treasure up and link with her dear name;
And a rude picture, so unlike the real,
It pleased me best to fancy an ideal
Of what she was, and send Thought softly back
To meet her, bounding over Memory's track.

But, oh! how like a vision from the skies
Now dawns on me the light of those dear eyes!
How my pulse quickens as those lips of flame
Seem waiting my approach, to breathe my name!
The silken lashes, brow and cheek so clear,
And sunny tresses too, all, all are here!
Ah! Heaven forgive me if I dare to bow
To idol such as this, and teach me how
To hush my spirit, that expectant waits,
And flaps her pinions 'gainst her prison-gates,
Impatient to be gone.   This mirrored face
Seems sent to comfort me—to fill her place;
To sit beside me in my silent room,
As was her wont, and cheat me of my gloom.

Artist, I love my lyre, and though each strain
That wakes beneath my touch may sleep again
Without evoking a responsive thrill
From other hearts, I love to sound it still.
But, were I called my treasure to resign
And choose a rarer gift, it would be thine,
The inspiration of thy magic Art;
The power to soothe and thrill the yearning heart.

OUT OF THE ARK.

COMPOSED FOR AND SUNG BY MRS. JOHN WYCOFF, DURING
THE REVIVAL MEETINGS AT KEOKUK, IOWA.

THEY recked not of danger, those scoffers of old,
    Whom Noah was chosen to warn;
From constant transgression their hearts had grown cold,
    And they answered his pleadings with scorn.
Yet daily he called, "Oh, come, sinners, come!
    Believe and prepare to embark;
Receive his kind message, and know there is room
    For all who will fly to the ark.
Then come! oh, come! oh, come!
    There's refuge alone in the ark."

They were not persuaded; unheeding they stood,
    Unmoved by his warning and prayer,
Till the prophet passed in from the oncoming flood,
    And left them to hopeless despair.
The flood-gates were open, the deluge came on,
    While Heaven, offended, grew dark;

They turned when too late : every foothold was gone ;
   And they perished in sight of the ark.
Too late, too late, too late !
   They perished in sight of the ark.

O sinners ! the heralds of mercy implore ;
   They cry, like the patriarch, "Come !"
The old ship of Zion is moored on your shore ;
   Her captain declares there is room.
The faithful have warned, believers have prayed,
   Yet you cling to the sin-deadened host ;
And soon of your perishing souls will be said,
   They listened, refused, and were lost,—
Were lost, were lost, were lost !
   Hear, sinner, your doom—they were lost !

EIGHTEEN HUNDRED AND FIFTY-NINE.

Oh, a grand old vessel was Fifty-Nine,
    And a captain brave had she;
For eighteen hundred and more stout ships
    He had steered over life's rough sea.
Eighteen hundred and more stout ships,
    Bound not for different goals,
But all for the same, and freighted down
    With cargoes of human souls.

And some of these souls were seared by crime;
    Some, sin had made foul and black;
While others were pure as the flakes of snow
    That cover our wild-flower track.
There were souls of monarchs, and souls of kings,
    (The souls of their subjects, too;)
And some were treacherous, false, and vile,
    While others were heavenly true.

There were souls of brokers, bare, flinty things,
    All shaved to the very core,

For even their honor was loaned on time,
   At a hundred per cent. or more.
There were coquettes' souls of chameleon dyes,
   And bachelors', knotty as pine,
And these unsocial and selfish souls
   Came alone to old Fifty-Nine.

And old Captain Time, as they came aboard,
   Counted all he could see ;
But some were so narrow and shriveled up,
   That they smuggled their passage free.

It was noon of night when the ship was launched,
   But the ocean was calm and clear ;
And merrily on, with her motley crew,.
   Went dancing the proud New Year.
On, past the glaciers of snow and ice
   That decked the receding shore ;
On to the isles where the spring-time sleeps,
   Till she hears Time's distant oar.

And the forests woke when they heard afar
   The flutter of coming sails ;
And whispered softly a low salute,
   That was borne by the passing gales.
And every eye on the vessel's deck
   Was turned toward that vision bright ;

And those who worshiped at Nature's shrine
   Were thrilled with a wild delight.

For those isles looked fair as a gleam of heaven
   Through the sunset's golden bars ;
Or like beauty's cheek, when its mantling flush
   Is seen by the light of stars.

The ship was moored where the gentle flowers
   Breathed fragrance on all around,
And the hours to some of the host within
   Brought blessings and peace profound.
But, hark ! from the deck of old Fifty-Nine
   A shout of defiance comes ;
Then the tramp of feet, and the clang of war,
   And the roll of advancing drums.

" To arms !" is echoed, in thunder-tones,
   Through the din of the cannon's roar ;
While sword and spear and the fair green earth
   Are sated with human gore.
But Captain Time says never a word
   To still the contending foes ;
He has promised to steer the ship to port,
   And has no hours to lose.

He is out, 'mid the blast and the shivering sails,
  Tolling the funeral bell,
And every soul that can hear the sound
  Sighs at the parting knell.
It tolls for one who has journeyed far,
  Whose labors a world may boast ;
Who has trodden Atlantic's crowded shore
  And Pacific's quiet coast ;

Whose wanderings led him o'er Southern plains,
  Where eternal sunshine sleeps ;
And up to the loftiest Alpine height
  Through snow-drifts' 'wildering steeps.
But Life's work is done, and the mourners pause
  That the billows his dirge may sing,
As the dust of Humboldt is laid to rest
  On the breast of the gentle Spring.

And slowly now is the vessel turned
  From those bright, enchanting isles,
To hasten on where the Summer waits
  With her witching, sunny smiles.
And it is not strange that those saddened hearts
  Grew light as they neared her bowers,
And caught the gleam of her azure robes
  Begirt with a zone of flowers ;

Or that Captain Time, though his form is bent,
  With labor and age and care,
Should feel a thrill through his palsied frame
  When his ship was anchored there;
That the hoary seaman should half forget
  The weight of unnumbered years,
When her rippling laugh, through ten thousand rills,
  Was borne to his agéd ears.

But see! as they coast round those India isles,
  Where the flowers of the orange blow,
Where the bulbul warbles its vesper hymns
  By the light of the fire-fly's glow,
With the speed of thought he has left her side,
  And fair Summer stands alone:
For off to the aft of old Fifty-Nine
  Was a sound like a dying groan.

He has reached the spot, and he chants this dirge
  As they bear the dust to shore,
And lay it down in its lonely bed
  With a sigh of "Nevermore":

"Toll! toll! for a mighty soul
  Is anchored in harbor now;
A mind creative, whose giant thoughts
  Made men to his genius bow.

K*

"Old Fifty-Nine, you are not so strong
   Since you yielded up this prize;
You will feel no more his sustaining arm
   When feuds and dissensions rise.
He will slumber here while incense sweet
   From the date- and the palm-tree float;
And a nation will hold in its heart of hearts
   The name of the statesman Choate.

"But reef the topsail! we may not wait
   To sigh o'er the mighty dead,
For I know, from the surge of yon mountain waves,
   There are breakers and shoals ahead.
Now cheerily, lads! though the billows dash,
   And the morrow bring cloudy weather,
We can bring her through with her motley crew
   If we only 'pull together.'"

And onward now, where grave Autumn sits
   In her scarlet robes and golden,
And presses the juice from the purple grape
   Like matrons in vineyards olden;
Where the blushing fruit from the ardent gaze
   Of the sun drops down, to cover
The deepening flush that might else betray
   Her heart to her distant lover:—

To this calm retreat Time hastens on,
　　To rest with the Autumn sober,
To gaze awhile on the cloudless skies
　　Of her dreamy, bright October.
But, hist! there's an echo borne to his ear,
　　Too feeble for distant thunder;
A sound as if fiends on old Fifty-Nine
　　Were tearing her shrouds asunder.

He turns and gazes; no fleet of war
　　Has fired a signal warning;
He sees no speck upon sea or sky
　　On that fair autumnal morning.
And yet—'tis strange (he is very old,
　　And, perchance, he is frail and doting)—
But he fancies he sees the timbers shake
　　Where the Flag of the Free is floating.

And he thinks he hears (what absurd conceits
　　Make mortals unfit to reason!)—
He thinks he hears in that muffled sound
　　A murmur of "Death and Treason."
Yet he breathes no word of his doubts and fears,
　　Lest they call it imagination,
Until night comes on, and he finds the clan
　　At their murderous preparation.

And he looks aghast at the horrid work
   The shadows of darkness cover,—
On the thirsty band that, like birds of prey,
   O'er their slumbering victims hover.
And with scorn he turns from those dastard souls,
   Their mutinous schemes bewailing,
While thought flies off to the days agone,
   When old Fifty-Two was sailing.

And he thinks of one of its gallant crew,
   Of his words of prophetic warning,
And sighs in vain for a Webster heart,
   With patriot fervor burning.
"But, true hearts, rouse ye," the captain cries,
   As the tars from their hammocks spring;
"We have traitors here we must urge to stay,
   Till we let them off—with a swing."

And once again is the vessel turned,
   To stem the boisterous gales
That blow from the bleak December's shore
   And moan through the shivering sails.
And hundreds of souls are landed here
   On this coast so drear and bare,
While some are left on the vessel's deck
   With looks of mute despair;

For they see their captain's form on shore,
    Afar o'er the waters wide,
And know that the ship is dashing on
    To eternity's waiting tide.
And if ye list, at the dead of night,
    To learn what her fate may be,
Ye may hear the wail of old Fifty-Nine
    As she sinks in that soundless sea.

20

THE FLAG OF THE FREE.

Oh, say! did you hear, 'mid the tempest of War,
  That swept like a blight through the heart of our
      Nation,
The soft whisper of Peace as it floated afar,
  Like an angel of Love, amid strife's desolation?
        Did you catch up the sound
        As it floated around?
  The word that from hill-side to vale should resound?
If so, hasten on to our grand Jubilee,
And rally in peace round the Flag of the Free.

'Neath its wide-spreading wing did the dauntless go forth,
  Where the fife and the drum drowned their hearts'
      muffled beating ;
Left the fagots ablaze on the love-hallowed hearth,
  A Father's kind care for their dear ones entreating.
        For they sprang at the cry,
        Without pause or reply,
  That bade them go forward to conquer or die.
And, with colors afloat, on the land and the sea,
They fought for their rights and the Flag of the Free.

Oh! grandly they stood, 'neath the Stripes and the Stars,
　　Undaunted by those who their Freedom rejected;
And proudly it waved, 'mid the conflict of Wars,
　　Untrailed and upheld, as by Heaven protected.
　　　　For dead patriots were there,
　　　　Bending o'er them in air,　　　　　　　.
　　And guarding our banner with tenderest care.
And 'twas these held the standard, that faint hearts
　　　　might see
The heaven-mirrored blue in the Flag of the Free.

Then, Sons of Columbia, in concert come forth,
　　And kneel where was purchased your Country's salva-
　　　　tion;
From the wide-spreading West to the life-teeming North
　　Let "Many in One" be the pledge of our Nation.
　　　　Oh! heed, one and all,
　　　　This Centennial call,
　　" United we stand but divided we fall."
And our Country's proud Banner in triumph will wave
O'er the Land of the Free and the Home of the Brave.

THE FOLLOWING ARE

POEMS

SELECTED FROM THE WRITINGS OF

PROFESSOR N. R. SMITH,

FATHER OF THE AUTHOR OF THIS VOLUME.

20*

APOSTROPHE TO THE GALAXY.

WHAT are ye, arrayed in your robings of white,
Beyond where the sun drinks in oceans of light;
Surmounting the stars, ay, the farthest we see
Just penciling heaven to prove that ye be?
A cluster so dreamy, expanding, and fair
Creates in the mind a fond wish to be there.
Your orbit our vision can never descry:
What are ye, in fleecy attiring on high?

Bright orbs, do ye give to the comet its ray,
Careering through space with impetuous sway?
Or, destined as vigils, watch over expanse,
To guard other worlds from the comet's advance?
So clustering are ye, so dense in your path,
Ye may save this fair earth from the wanderer's wrath.

What are ye? Oh, say, does your circuit extend
Round orbs where the angels their minstrelsy blend?
And do ye pour forth on the throng and the choir
The splendor of light from the disk of your fire?
If such be your destiny, Galaxy bright,
The music how rapturous, blended with light!

Like the songs of the spheres when the Deity's voice
In the light of creation made angels rejoice.

What are ye?   If not what the muse has defined,
Then are ye not orbits of beautiful mind?
Are the white, stainless robes ye expand to our view
In chasteness the emblems of mind among you?
In fancy's excursions behold I not there
In your orbs so resplendent, your region so fair,
Intelligence, rising by intellect's force
Still nearer to Him, of perfection the source,
With natures immortal, all spotless in soul,
And cherishing mind, as in splendor ye roll?

Behold I not, grouped round your altars of praise,
Your children, at even, their orisons raise?
Or, cheerful and happy, in youth's ardent glow,
All sporting in fields where the wild-flowers grow?
A father bends over his boy with a smile,
A mother caresses her infant the while;
Joy blended with joy, and bliss mingled with bliss,
In the fond interchange of a smile and a kiss.

Methinks I can see, by your rills and bland streams,
Your poets, entranced in elysian dreams,
Or, waked from their raptures among your green bowers,
Rehearsing their numbers while culling the flowers;

The learned of your system—philosophers wise,
Astronomers, mapping the stars of *your* skies,
Vast oceans expanding, your landscapes serene,
Your redolent groves and your valleys of green.

If systems of mind ye are not, still the word,
What are ye?   No answer but echo is heard.
Do ye lead in the van of the spheres as they whirl?
Is the vision of whiteness the flag ye unfurl?
And, on the reverse, are there emblems displayed
Of orbs in full splendor and glory arrayed?

Whate'er ye may seem to our dim, mortal view,
Bright star-isles that gleam in your ocean of blue,
We will deem you a stellar assemblage refined,
And with you compare the bright grouping of mind,
To show how it can, like the stars, by its glow,
Relieve our life's orb from the gloom of its woe.

ANTICIPATION AND POSSESSION.

WHY do we grieve when fancied joys
    Elude our grasp and fly?
If ever, we should mourn when flits
    Some dread reality.

Should Hope's delusions mar our bliss,
    'Tis folly to bewail
The wreck of Fancy's brightest dreams,
    When what we *have* is frail.

What though to-day a thousand gems
    In flattering prospect rise?
What though to-morrow every one
    Elude our ravished eyes?

Should Reason prompt us to repine
    For what was ne'er our own?
Or rather, will it not reprove
    Our grief for bliss unknown?

What can Hope's sunny visions yield,
  Her fairest beamings lend,
To vie with joys that round our homes
  In sweet assemblage blend ?

Is not the spell that Woman casts
  More bland to heart and eye
Than all the promises of Hope,
  Or Fancy's imagery ?

Our little ones,—do they not win
  Our bosoms' warmest zeal ?
What sweeter than the pledge of love
  Can dreams of bliss reveal ?

Our friends,—do not their smiles enhance
  The joys that we possess ?
Do not their greetings sweeten life,
  And make its sorrows less ?

Yet these endeared realities
  May leave us in a day ;
Far wiser, then, to have and love,
  And mourn when they decay.

THE FEAST OF THE FAIRIES.

ONE holy-night the fays convened,
  All in full mirth and glee;
And formed a gay, fantastic ring
  To Zephyrs' minstrelsy.

The fairy-dance went round and round,
  All merriment and sheen,
Till one fay o'er a moonbeam fell,
  And broke the magic scene.

And now 'twas feast-time; Fancy called
  Each airy-footed sprite;
And oh, the riot that prevailed
  Upon that festal night!

For Fancy, mistress of the spell,
  Presided o'er the cheer;
And, at her beck, each joyous fay,
  With viands choice, drew near.

The dish that Love had ordered
  Proved a medley, tough and tart;
Among its contents she discerned
  A dry and shriveled heart.

It was a *bachelor's.* She tore
  And twisted, wrenched and wrung,—
At length she spurned the gristly thing,
  And then the fairies sung:

"A bachelor's heart does not belong
  To heaven or earth, we trow;
We'll toss it up, and we'll toss it down,
  And we'll toss it to and fro."

And then that heart, oh, how it flew
  The laughing fays among!
As football some the odd thing struck,
  And some with fury flung.

But Fancy frowned upon the scene,
  And, when the frolic ceased,
She mixed in one the dishes all,
  And spoiled the fairies' feast.

Oh, then, a pretty mess appeared!
  Smiles, kisses, hearts betrayed,

Forget-me-nots, and broken vows
   Were, in rude plight, displayed.

The elves they had not feasted yet,
   Shrill chanticleer crowed—one ;
The moon withdrew her golden beams,—
   The fairy-feast was done.

But ere they parted, though provoked
   At Fancy's churlish ire,
They sang the song they'd sung before,
   And Zephyrs joined the choir :

" A bachelor's heart does not belong
   To heaven or earth, we trow ;
We'll toss it up, and we'll toss it down,
   And we'll toss it to and fro."

FLOWERS.

WHO loves not flowers?—a forest in its dress
Of verdure, rich with figures colored bright?
Not gaudily, but with such hues as press
With a soft, mellow touch upon the sight,
Wooing the vision's love.

     'Tis art alone
Yields gaudy tints to flowers by culture, which
Dame Nature ne'er employs when they are grown
In fields and forests; there they put forth rich,
Indeed, but unassuming forms, with cups
For dew and odors for the zephyrs. Naught
Intrudes there, nothing rude that interrupts
The plastic course of Nature; all is wrought,
The smallest flower expanding, to emit
Unsullied fragrance, pure ambrosial drops,
Reflecting colors, by its structure fit
To enchain the mind in thought. The storm crops
Not a blossom, laying the forest bare;
From among the ruins every flower looks
Blooming still without a nurse's care,
Save Nature, to protect it; and the brooks,

Though cumbered with the fragments, still gush free
To bathe the violet's head, lest Sol's fierce ray
Might else the floweret sear.

                    In childhood's glee,
When my light spirits bubbled up in play,
I thought with Darwin lovely flowers could feel,
Were sentient beings, and could laugh or weep.
It was my wont to sit for hours, or steal
Around to see the florid things asleep,
Or, waking up, give forth a cheerful smile
After a pleasant nap.   Thus to employ
My time, or much of it, did oft beguile
With rosy bliss the too confiding boy.
Yet 'twas not all illusion.   Years mature,
With notice and research, conviction brought,
That flowers at night enjoy repose, secure
From harm, as if the blooming gems were taught
By Nature to seek rest, awake as we,
Refreshed, and with the morn expand in bloom.
  Who loves not flowers?   At morn and noon, the bee
Within their nectaries, while they perfume
The air, sips honey for the hive, the boon
Imparted freely as the light of day;
And thus do flowers instruct us to attune
The heart to such emotions as display

Unstinted charity from private means,
And while we thus in secret give, around
Diffuse benevolence divine, which screens
The poor from wretchedness wherever found.

    Who loves not flowers? To study them, to learn
The use of every organ, how it plies
Its power instinctive to one end, discern
The avenues of health, and when it dies,
To see a flower resign to death its form
With all its loveliness; these to the mind
Impressive truths convey, the bosom warms
With pure devotion, feelings all refined.

    Who loves not flowers? 'Tis pleasant to converse
With them. As learned mutes their thoughts unfold
By signs, so Flora's pupils can rehearse
By symbols clear and cogent: they can mold
The callous heart so as to make it feel
The force of virtue, can convince, reclaim
The inward and the outward man, reveal
What Inspiration urges as the aim,
Design, and reason of our living here;
And thus with Heaven's own Book of faith and love,
Unite in yielding proof direct and clear
Of life hereafter. Then, who loves not flowers?

O! AND OH!

O! THE enchanting hues that rise
  To deck the morn's young features!
Oh! see what clouds obscure the skies!
  Oh! back! ye gloomy creatures!

O! who's the churl that can refrain
  From prospects so delightful!
Oh! tempest! lightning! thunder! rain!
  How dreary! Oh! how frightful!

O! pleasant 'tis at sea to view
  The bright horizon round you!
Oh! where's the ship! The storms burst through!
  The raging waves have found you!

O! grateful are the strains that pour
  From every grove and bower!
Oh! quaking is that thunder's roar!
  It comes with deafening power!

O ! blooming as the rosy skies
   That fair one's glowing beauty !
Oh ! loathsome those cadaverous eyes !
   Complexion ! Oh ! how sooty !

O ! how that form regales the sense !
   What symmetry is given !
Oh, ugly, graceless being, hence !
   Earth claims thee not nor heaven !

O ! what a boon, in weal or woe,
   Is health, life's fairest etching !
Oh ! oh ! this pain ! this sickness ! Oh !
   Oh ! oh ! this morbid retching !

O ! favored they who never want
   The man of pills to call up !
Oh ! torturing bolus ! oh ! avaunt,
   This calomel and jalap !

O friends ! how true ! Oh, foes, how base !
   O wealth ! Oh, hard dependence !
O blest abode ! Oh, wretched place,
   With all its vile attendants !

And thus in O's! our pleasures flow;
  In Ohs! our pains; Oh! galling!
But some—'tis wrong—use Oh! for O!
  And O! for Oh! appalling!

A TEMPERANCE SONG FOR THE FOURTH OF JULY.

TUNE.—"ROSE OF ALLANDALE."

A VOICE is heard upon the gale,
　　Shrill joy it bears along;
From city, hamlet, hill and dale,
　　Bursts forth the welcome song.
And echo sends it, long and loud,
　　Through all the land with glee;
Upon the air glad voices crowd,
　　Proclaiming—WE ARE FREE.

The cup that foamed with deadly bane
　　Is dashed upon the ground.
'Twas death to millions at the fane
　　Where misery was found.
An angel near that Dagon drew,
　　She bade the prisoners flee,
And sent the pledge the nation through
　　Proclaiming—THEY ARE FREE.

1.*

The mother's heart with joy beats high,
   Her son's no more a wreck ;
The beam of hope is in her eye,
   His arms around her neck.
A freeman, him her bosom claims
   With all a mother's glee,
"My child !" her raptured tongue exclaims,
   " My child ! my boy is free !"

And freemen such, this day, in throngs
   To country homage pay ;
They welcome Freedom by their songs
   On this, her holy-day.
Then let the temperance flag, unfurled,
   Our country's standard be ;
And wave this motto to the world,
   " Columbia is free !"

OLD SOLDIERS.

WE love the spot where Valor bled
   In the days of other years;
Where some young hero bowed his head
   Whom memory endears.

We venerate the mound where lie
   Some agéd veteran's bones;
Though naught denotes his victory
   But rude unsculptured stones.

Say not the Revolution's age
   In memory has no place:
· Because the present has its page,
   The former to efface!

Old soldiers, those who yet remain,
   Oh! guard with tenderest care;
Remembering that they sowed the seed
   That made us what we are.

Prop up those withered oaks that stand,
   Memorials of the past:
They tell and point, with trembling hand,
   Where Liberty was cast;

Tell where the hero Washington
   With his compatriots trod;
Where many a dauntless warrior's soul
   Passed up from strife to God.

Then let our grateful homage prove
   Our true fidelity,
To those whose valor, honor, love,
   Were pledged to make us free.

THE END,

MEMORIAL HALL.

1776   AGRICULTURAL BUILDING.   1876.

MACHINERY HALL.

INTERNATIONAL EXHIBITION

PHILADELPHIA U.S. AMERICA

MAY 10TH TO NOVEMBER 10TH 1876

HORTICULTURAL HALL.

WOMEN'S PAVILION.